BULL'S-EYE
IN BUCKEYE

Buckeye Springs, Kansas. It should have been a peaceful little town. But it wasn't.

A gang of pro-slavers was sweeping in to burn it to the ground in the most brutal orgy of destruction that the battle-torn territory had ever seen.

A ragtag army led by a woman as brave under fire as she was fiery under a man's kisses was lined up against it.

And one gun spelled the difference between bloody victory and bloody defeat.

It belonged to Canyon O'Grady, hair-triggered for trouble, with orders to stop the slaughter by shooting to kill . . .

CANYON O'GRADY

8

BLEEDING KANSAS

by

Jon Sharpe

A SIGNET BOOK

SIGNET
Published by the Penguin Group Penguin Books USA Inc.,
375 Hudson Street, New York, New York 10014, U.S.A.
Penguin Books Ltd, 27 Wrights Lane, London W8 5TZ, England
Penguin Books Australia Ltd, Ringwood, Victoria, Australia
Penguin Books Canada Ltd, 2801 John Street,
Markham, Ontario, Canada L3R 1B4
Penguin Books (N.Z.) Ltd, 182-190 Wairau Road, Auckland 10, New Zealand

Penguin Books Ltd, Registered Offices: Harmondsworth, Middlesex, England

First published by Signet, an imprint of Penguin Books USA Inc.

First Printing, July, 1990
10 9 8 7 6 5 4 3 2 1

The first chapter of this book previously appeared in *The King of Colorado*,
the seventh volume in this series.

 REGISTERED TRADEMARK—MARCA REGISTRADA

Printed in the United States of America

PUBLISHER'S NOTE
This is a work of fiction. Names, characters, places, and incidents either are
the product of the author's imagination or are used fictitiously, and any resem-
blance to actual persons, living or dead, events, or locales is entirely coinci-
dental.

Canyon O'Grady

His was a heritage of blackguards and poets, fighters and lovers, men who could draw a pistol and bed a lass with the same ease.

Freedom was a cry seared into Canyon O'Grady, justice a banner of his heart.

With the great wave of those who fled to America, the new land of hope and heartbreak, solace and savagery, he came to ride the untamed wildness of the Old West.

With a smile or a six-gun, Canyon O'Grady became a name feared by some and welcomed by others, but remembered by all . . .

Buckeye Springs, Kansas, August 1858.
New territories Kansas and Nebraska
are up for grabs—free or slave?
Emotions run high, violence is rampant.
Kansas is bleeding . . .

1

Hattie Stover narrowed her eyes and spat out the words at the woman who held the front of her jacket in a tight grip. "You're nothing but another one of them damn southerners who should have stayed down South. You think you're so much better than the rest of us. You think you can turn all of the rest of us into your slaves. You're a lackey of the devil, you are, you—you hussy!"

Beth Jo Tolliver tightened her grip on Hattie's jacket and twisted. "And you're a bible-spouting whore who don't deserve this fine Kansas Territory. Why don't you go back to Illinois, where you can spout your narrow brand of religion with them other nigger-loving cowards."

Tabitha Rothmore hurried to the pair and scowled at both women. "Enough," she bellowed in an unladylike manner. "Let go of each other or I'll dump a bucket of water on you both. Now!"

Neither woman moved. Tabitha brought her clenched fist down sharply on Beth Jo's wrist and the woman screeched in pain and let go. Tabitha pushed her back a step.

"This is a retail establishment, not a public forum or bare-knuckled fistfight parlor," Tabitha said, trying to control her temper. "I allow no political discussions in here. If either of you wish to make a purchase or just shop, fine. If you want to continue this unladylike brawl, you'll have to do it out in the street with the other ruffians."

Hattie glared at the other woman, turned, and picked up the new frying pan she had come for and went to the counter. Beth Jo fumed for a moment, then turned and flounced out of the store. She stormed past two men who were jawing at each other on the way in.

"Hell, I don't care what you say. I don't want no damn southerner running a hundred slaves on his place down the road from me. What good's a bunch of slaves gonna do here? Can't raise cotton in Kansas. Wheat and corn and steers, that's what we raise. How many men can you use to pick sixty acres of corn?"

"You're just ignorant. Don't got to have a hundred slaves. Hell, ten or fifteen would do fine for a small-size farm. I plan on buying me ten of them as soon as the state goes slave in the election."

"Stupid as you are, Harvey, you might not live that long."

"Yeah? Says who, bastard?"

The two men turned to face each other, their hands near the guns in the leather holsters on their hips. Neither man knew much about his newly acquired revolver, but each figured a weapon was a requirement these days in Kansas.

Both hesitated.

"Hell, Harvey, you're too yellow-bellied to draw."

"I already drew, gents," Tabitha called to them from ten feet away. "This is a double-barreled scatter-gun with double-ought buck. Got me a round for each of you. No gunplay in my store except by me. Now keep your hands over your heads and both of you get out of my store. This ain't no damn debating society. I found my pa hung just outside this store one morning, killed by men like you. I'm not taking any guff off any of you. No more. I can pull a trigger damn good. You two want to find out? Later, if you want to come back and buy something, fine. Now out!"

Both men lifted their hands and backed toward the door. They hated to look into the loaded barrel of a shotgun. Death lurked there only a trigger pull away, and they knew it. The two men made it to the door and scurried in opposite directions down the street.

A minute later a tall man with a mustache and cropped-close beard walked into the store. He pulled off his town hat, revealing dark-brown hair flecked with gray. His eyes were cold green, a tin star decorated his vest.

"Seems you had some differences with those two men," Sheriff Loughran said. "They came out of here with their hands up."

"This store ain't a public place. I don't allow no politics talked here. And no fighting or gunplay either. Any law against that?"

Loughran laughed wryly. " 'Course not, Miss Rothmore, 'course not. Just checking."

"While you're checking why don't you find the degenerate who hung my pa? That's what you should be doing."

"Like I told you a month ago, Miss Rothmore, there's just no way to be sure which side did the hanging. For sure there was no evidence and no witnesses. I can't make the rope talk."

Tabitha Rothmore gave a big sigh and tried to catch her breath. Two fights in a row in her general store, she thought. Things had been getting worse here in Buckeye Springs. It wasn't like it was the territorial capital or anything. Why all this politics? Who cared if the state was slave or free?

Tabitha eyed the sheriff of Ashland County. "Something I can get for you, Sheriff Loughran?"

"Nope, just wondered about that pair you run out. Hear you put a pistol through the ceiling yesterday to end an argument. Pistol is one thing, a damn shotgun is another."

Tabitha looked down and saw that she still held the shotgun. "Wasn't cocked, Sheriff. I know about guns."

As she turned, Loughran watched with appreciation the trim ankle that showed under the flare of her calico dress. Her waist nipped in sharply and he saw that her bodice pulled tight over her generous breasts.

"Thanks for checking, Sheriff," she said, turning to look at him over one slender shoulder. Loughran nodded at her. Tabitha's blond hair hung just to her shoulders. She said she kept it that short because she didn't have an hour a day to comb and brush and curl it. The straight bangs over her soft-blue eyes had grown almost to the eyebrow-covering stage.

Her chin was firm and strong and her cheekbones wide and high. Her face had a pretty look, but not one that would be confused with classic beauty.

"I've got to price and put out some things, Sheriff."

"Go right ahead."

"You don't seem to get mixed up in the slave/free issue," Tabitha said.

"Can't. I've got to be impartial."

"But isn't there something you can do about these house burnings and the killings?"

"We try, Miss Rothmore, but I've only got one deputy. There's no chance I can keep up with all the arson, let alone a man shot dead here and there. We try."

She nodded.

"Guess I better see what's happening up and down the street." Sheriff Loughran put on his hat, touched her brim, and walked out the front door.

Tabitha marked the prices on the goods just in from Chicago. Most folks hadn't thought she'd be able to run the store with her pa gone. She had been determined to make a go of the business, and now, a month later, it was doing better than ever. She had helped her pa run the store ever since her ma died three years ago.

She had known from the very first that her pa had not been hung by either the pro-slave folks or the free-state people. Her pa didn't take sides in politics. Nobody had a reason to hurt him.

That was why she'd written three letters to the territorial capital. One went to the attorney general, one to the governor, and one to the head of the U.S. marshals for this section of the country.

She had been surprised when a marshal had come into town a week after she sent the letter. He talked with her and then with half a dozen other people the first day he was there. But then, that night, he got into an argument with somebody in the Hell Hole Saloon.

There had been one of those fast, spur-of-the-moment shoot-outs, and when it was over, the marshal lay dead on the floor. That had been the final blow for Tabitha. She figured the same people who killed her pa had also killed the marshal. She decided that the marshal's death would be the end of it. She had been right. She hadn't seen or heard from anyone else in the marshal's office or the territorial capital.

So, she had dug in hard at the store, working fourteen, sometimes sixteen hours a day to make it the best, most-up-to-date retail establishment in town. More women were coming in these days to look at pictures, dishes, household things, and now and then, wallpaper.

Tabitha didn't want to let her father's murder drop, but she had no idea what to do. She wanted desperately to find and punish whoever killed her pa, but she didn't know how. She wiped a bead of perspiration off her forehead with the sleeve of her dress and walked to the front of the store as another customer came in.

Down the street in the Kansas Barber Shop, proprietor James Washington stropped his straight-edge razor to a fine edge and finished shaving the manager of the stagecoach station. He came in every week for a haircut and a shave.

"Should keep you safe for another week, Red," Washington said as he slapped a little bay rum and witch hazel on the man's cheeks and chin. Washington caught the quarter in payment, put it in his money drawer, and looked at the next customer. The man was the only other person in the shop.

"Kinole, you don't need a haircut," Washington said as he waved him to the chair.

"Make it look like it. I been hearing all sort of yackety from that little rancher out by the river. Nickler, Diego Nickler, is his name. He's a slave man and has been trying to get together a defense group."

Washington looked around the small barber shop. There was no one else who could hear. "Figure he's a good candidate for our new lodge?"

"Sooner the better. The little bastard is a loudmouth."

"Tonight be too early for you?" Washington asked.

Kinole grinned. "Hell, no. You better run the clippers around my ears and put the cloth over me. I saw somebody looking in the window a minute ago.'

Washington draped the cloth over Kinole, trimmed around his ears with the hand-operated hair clippers, and then fussed a bit with comb and scissors. He finished with a flurry of the bay rum and witch hazel and patted Kinole's cheeks.

"What time?" Kinole asked.

"Usual. Midnight. Let's meet at the old icehouse. It's damn near empty now. We'll need horses."

Kinole watched Washington. "You think this is doing some good?"

"Damn right. We're chasing some of the big mouths out of the county. Shutting up a few. Hell, a man loses his barn or his house and it makes him do some thinking."

Washington flipped off the cloth and shook it as he always did, then motioned Kinole out of the chair. Washington dropped into the chair himself. He had hurting feet today. Twenty years of standing behind a barber chair didn't help naturally flat feet.

He had been a barber all his life. He was twenty pounds overweight, starting to bald on the top of his head, and had the sagging jowls of a man twenty years older. His brown eyes were constantly bloodshot; no problem with them, they just always looked that way. He was clean-shaven—in fact, when he had time, he shaved twice a day. He hated men with beards. Cut down on his business. His hands were long-fingered and clean. He washed them a dozen times a day.

"We ask the same three guys?" Kinole asked.

"Right. And be sure they wear dark clothes, bring a mask, and ride a dark horse. No more white horses like Carter rode the last time."

Kinole laughed. "I almost shot him myself." He waved and walked out of the barber shop. He had most of the afternoon to contact the three other men who would ride with them that night. He was a jeweler, and a damn good one, but in a town this size there was little to do besides repairing watches and winding up alarm clocks.

Washington watched Kinole go. He was a good field man; he knew a lot more people in the area than Washington did. Hell, nobody knew everyone. The town was only three years old—nobody had been allowed to settle in this part of the country until 1854. Washington had followed it closely. When Kansas and Nebraska were made territories by Congress, he had picked up from St. Louis and rushed out to Kansas, stopping at the first good-sized town he found. There was always work for a good barber.

Even today, Buckeye Springs wasn't that big, maybe five hundred people living in town, with four saloons, two general stores, a bunch of other stores, and a smattering of houses. He wasn't sure why the town grew up there. It was on a small stage route west, which helped.

Quickly Washington had found others in town who had come here to help Kansas become a free state. He had been told to do anything practical to keep Kansas in the free-soil list of states. He was doing just that.

The pro-slavery people were killing and burning. He and his team of eight men had not killed anyone yet, but they had a list of ten houses, barns, and other assorted buildings they had burned to the ground and at least fifty people they had scared.

Washington grinned. They were going to scare a whole lot more of the pro-slavery rednecks before this thing was over. Lately things were turning nasty. Three men that he knew of had been killed right there in the county. That wasn't counting Stan Rothmore. The general-store owner had no strong views. That killing was not a part of the blood feud about slavery. Washington would give odds on that.

He turned as a customer came into the shop. The man was one that he needed to talk to. They said their hellos, and the man settled into the barber chair for a light trim.

"Don't work up any important meetings for tonight," Washington said. "We've got a little ride to take along about midnight."

The man in the chair turned and grinned. "Great! I've been waiting for you to give the call."

2

Canyon O'Grady watched President James Buchanan flip the hand-tied fishing fly back and forth on the springy fly rod and then sail the small light fly twenty feet out into the swiftly flowing stream. Gradually the president worked the fly back up the current and into the edge of a deep pool.

A moment later there was a splashing froth as a golden trout leapt out of the water with the fly in its mouth and splashed back in, hooked by a quick pull on the line by the president.

The fish took off downstream and the line on the president's reel hummed for a minute, then slowed as he fought the two-pounder. He worked him back into quieter waters, wading up to his knees in the mountain stream before bringing him close enough to lure into a hand-held net.

The president lifted the fish and showed him to O'Grady. "What a beauty! That's a golden trout, O'Grady. One of the finest fighting fish in the world. They also are called sunapee, and are of the general salmon genus. Your turn, give it a try."

O'Grady swept the fly back and forth twice, the way he had seen the president do it, then he laid it out a dozen feet in front of him. He had only begun to pull the fly upstream in gentle tugs when a fish struck and he had all he could do to best the trout in the struggle. When O'Grady at last pulled the fish into the shallows and lifted him from the water and carried the flopping creature to shore, he saw that it was much smaller than the one the president had caught.

"Well done, O'Grady, well done. I knew I picked the right man for this trip. Now, let's get back to camp and have the cook fix these for our midday lunch. You're due to ride out by two o'clock so you can make your train connections. Has anyone told you what the small problem is that we have for you this time?"

"No, Mr. President, nobody has said a word."

President James Buchanan smiled. His deep-set eyes danced with mirth. It was one of the few times O'Grady had seen the president even halfway happy. Usually he looked like he was packing the weight of the globe on his shoulders.

His starkly white hair showed even whiter now against his high forehead, which had taken on a bronzed glow from the sun.

"Actually, I want you to stop the northern states from wrangling with the southern states." He glanced up at O'Grady and smiled. "But that's my job, so I won't pass it on. No, all you have to worry about is Kansas. Some friends of mine say that Kansas is bloody and in chaos. Practically a civil war with organizations, and battles fought and towns taken and then lost, and prisoners released.

"Mixed into this pro/anti-slavery brouhaha is another problem that may or may not be related. We've had a U.S. marshal shot to death in the back and made out like it was a straight Wild West gunfight.

"I want you to go out there and straighten out the mess. One of my men will have a package for you, a thin one. But it will give you all the information we have. Now, let's watch the cook pan-fry those trout over an open fire. This was a dandy idea, coming up here for a week's rest."

The two men sat on a blanket spread on the grass under some trees as they watched the cook work over the trout and drop the cleaned fish into a skillet on an open fire.

"Canyon, I worked damned hard to get this job. Now some days I don't know if I want it or not. The southerners are now calling me an abolitionist, and the northerners are calling me pro-slavery. Seems I can't win.

"My big job in this office was to bring the fighting halves of this country together. Even before I got the nomination, I worked hard to do just enough for the South so they would approve of me and help me get the party's nod. I don't deny that.

"Hell, I opposed the Wilmot Proviso in 1846 that would prohibit slavery in U.S. territories. I voted for a bill excluding antislavery literature going in the U.S. mail. I even supported the 1850 Compromise that tried to maintain a balance of U.S. Senate seats between the free and slave states.

"Now, don't get me wrong, O'Grady. I thought then, and I still think now, that slavery is morally wrong, repugnant. But I wanted to show the South that I respect the constitutional safeguards for their way of life down there.

"I even had a big part in drafting the Ostend Manifesto in 1854. You might not remember it. The manifesto was a diplomatic report recommending the U.S. acquisition of Cuba from Spain. We were trying to forestall any chance of a slave uprising in Cuba. We figured that it would splash over into the South and we might have a bloody slave uprising of our own.

"Well, I finally convinced enough of the southern party members I wouldn't outlaw slavery, and I got nominated and then elected. Now sometimes I wonder if I can make any difference in this epic struggle at all. This country seems hell-bent toward a blow-up over slavery, and I don't know what form it's going to take.

"Kansas could just be one spot where things get so out of hand that it would trigger a war. I don't know. See what you can do out there. I know it's a mess. I've thought of sending in federal troops often enough. I've talked with the Kansas territorial governor about calling out the Kansas militia. So far we have used troops both sparingly and with care.

"Well, now, it looks as if those trout are done. Fish don't take long to cook. Mind the bones now. Best way is to try to split the cooked fish and lift out the backbone and the ribs all in one piece."

A day and a half later, O'Grady sat in a train heading for St. Louis, Missouri. For the third time during the trip, O'Grady spread out the papers on the seat beside him and started to read as the land flashed by at thirty miles an hour. He was getting used to traveling by trains. Sure beat riding a stagecoach or a horse.

The first report he read came from the marshal's office.

> This office had a letter two months ago about the death of one Stanley Rothmore, 46, of Buckeye Springs, Kansas Territory. Rothmore was the proprietor of a general store that also contained the town's post office. He was postmaster for the small town, which makes his death an official matter for this office.
>
> Rothmore was hanged late one night from the front of his store, which has a second-floor section that extends beyond the sidewalk. He was found the next morning by citizens and cut down. Kansas is in the middle of a tremendous struggle over the slavery/antislavery issue. However it was resolved that Rothmore was not involved with either side and had never made his beliefs on the matter public in any way. He refused even to talk about the problems.
>
> Rothmore's daughter wrote urging us to investigate the death, wanting his killer brought to justice.
>
> We dispatched a U.S. marshal, J. B. Tippit, to the scene. Before he had a chance to report back to our Omaha office, he was shot and killed in the Hell Hole Saloon in Buckeye Springs.
>
> A week after his death, we were notified by the

sheriff there, Harry Loughran, who said the death appeared to have occurred as the result of an argument in a saloon and a subsequent gunfight that by the accounts of the witnesses was a "fair fight."

A week after that report we had a curious letter from Gunnar Holtzer, the undertaker in Buckeye Springs. He reported that the dead man had one bullet wound that entered the body from the front, a shot through the side that gouged out no more than an inch of flesh. It would have been nonfatal.

The killing blow came from three large-caliber rounds that struck the victim from the back. One severed Tippit's spinal cord, a second punctured his right lung, and the third went through a lung and into Tippit's heart. Any of the three wounds would have resulted in death.

Holtzer's question was how could a "fair fight" be declared when the body had four bullet holes in it? Holtzer said he had not revealed this information to anyone else in town—not to the daughter, not to the sheriff, not to the doctor.

At this point we refrained from sending in another marshal, fearing for his life and wishing a more coordinated campaign to discover the truth about Buckeye Springs. We fear that Tippit's death was tied in with the slavery issue now taking a bloody toll in Kansas. There is a surge of violence and partisan activity in Buckeye Springs at this time.

We stand by ready to cooperate with any other agency or department. Please keep us informed."

The paper was signed by Colonel Wilson Marks, U.S. Marshal's Office, Omaha Division, Nebraska Territory.

O'Grady put down the papers and stared at them for a minute, then shuffled them together, put a clip on them, and pushed them back in the big brown envelope. There were two more bunches of papers for him to look through again. He had most of it memorized.

He stared out the window trying to assimilate the problem at hand. "Murder most foul" as the English would say. Why? Was Rothmore secretly the head of one of the slavery/antislavery factions? Was his death part of a larger plot to plunge Kansas into an all-out civil war?

Someone was walking down the aisle. Canyon watched the elderly woman moving slowly along as the train swayed gently around a curve. When the woman had passed, he saw an attractive lady sitting across from him. She glanced at him, then looked away at once.

Twice more in the next few minutes he saw her looking at him. She had thick dark-red hair that came halfway down her back. It was a burnished gold with highlights of softer shades. He guessed she was in her mid-twenties. She looked at him again and he smiled. She smiled back just for a moment, then looked away.

O'Grady put the rest of his papers in the envelope and hooked his suit coat in his thumb and moved across the aisle. "Miss, the coach is so crowded today, I wondered if you would mind if I sat here?"

There were two seats on that side of the aisle. She glanced up and grinned, an open, warm expression that made her green eyes sparkle. She hesitated for just a moment and he sat down beside her.

"Of course, the train is so crowded today." They both looked up and down the aisle where there were ten or twelve people in a car that would hold eighty. They laughed softly.

She held out her hand. "I'm Meg Ryson."

"I'm Canyon O'Grady." They shook hands.

"Canyon? That's an unusual name."

"My mother liked it, but the parish priest in Ireland would have none of it and I was baptized Michael Patrick O'Grady. But my friends call me Canyon."

"I want to call you Canyon." She said it and then looked away.

"Are you traveling far?" he asked.

"To Kansas City. I have some relatives near there."

"We'll be to St. Louis in the morning," he said.

"I feel like I've been traveling for days," Meg said.

"Better than a stagecoach, which does take days. Fifty miles a day sometimes was all."

Meg smiled. "I guess I like this better. How far are you going?"

"Kansas City, and then south a ways. Business."

"Oh." She brightened her face into a smile. "I'm turning south at Kansas City as well. We can talk and make the time go faster."

"That sounds good. Where are you coming from?"

"Boston. I was there to go to school. Not that it will do me much good. My father has a husband all picked out for me, but I told him I wouldn't marry anyone unless I pick out the man."

O'Grady laughed. "Good girl. But here you are almost an old maid."

"Am not! I'm only twenty-two." Her voice took on a sharp tone and she frowned for a moment.

"Easy, lass. It looks like you have a wee bit of an Irish temper."

"My mother is Irish, my father English—twice removed, as he says. My great-grandmother way back sometime came over during the Revolutionary War as a lobsterback. He was billeted in a household and fell in love with the owner's daughter. He deserted the British army and married the girl."

"Beautiful, lusty girls were our best weapons against the British in that war," O'Grady said.

"But you must still have been in Ireland at the time. Or at least your ancestors, that is."

As they talked, learning more about each other, the daylight faded. There was a modest dining car and they both had sandwiches for supper and then went back to their seats. The train swayed just before they sat down and she fell hard against him. He caught her and held her tightly as the train straightened. Her breasts crowded against his chest and her face was an inch from his.

"Oh, my," Meg said. "This traveling can be dangerous."

O'Grady chuckled. "I'll take that kind of danger any day."

Meg smiled as they sat down. It was fully dark then. Only a small gaslight burned midway along in the car. Several of the passengers were sleeping already in the leaned-back coach seats.

She reached for his hand. He caught it and held, watching her. She leaned her head closer to his. "O'Grady, could I ask you a favor?"

"Of course. Anything for an old Irish colleen friend."

"Would you kiss me good night?"

"Am I leaving?"

"No, please stay. I thought you might want a nap."

"I never go to sleep when I'm this close to a beautiful sexy lady."

"Hush that talk and kiss me."

He did.

Her lips clung to his for a moment, then her mouth opened. It was a long kiss. When it ended, she sucked in a quick little gasp of pleasure.

"O'Grady, you did not learn that in schoolbooks."

"Nor did you, lass. We could try it again."

She leaned more to him this time, and in the darkness his hand fell on her breast and the kiss was hotter. His hand stayed on her breast.

"This is crazy," Meg said. "I don't know you at all. I'm kissing you like we've been courting for a year."

"A year and a half." Canyon slipped out of his suit coat and leaned toward her side of the seat, then draped the coat over them both around their shoulders. "That's to keep us warm."

"I'm having no trouble staying warm," Meg said. One of her hands strayed to his leg under the jacket. O'Grady's hand worked gently through the buttons of her blouse and she looked at him with a frown, then she lifted her brows and kissed his nose.

His hand closed around one of her bare breasts and she gasped, then smiled as he began to caress her.

Meg whispered in his ear. "Do you know what you're doing to me? Do you know how utterly wanton that makes me feel?" She kissed him with her mouth open and made soft noises in her throat. Her hand worked down between his legs and then came up and covered the hard swelling she found there.

O'Grady tweaked her nipple, massaged it until he could feel it lift and fill with hot, surging blood. Then he moved his hand to her other orb and Meg purred softly.

She leaned close to his ear. "O'Grady, undo those damn buttons for me or I'll die!"

He pushed one hand down and undid the buttons on his fly and then found her breasts again.

Someone walked down the aisle and they both remained quiet, with only deep, even breathing, as if they were sleeping. The footsteps passed on by without pausing.

"You're a beast, O'Grady, getting me all worked up this way and letting me simmer. Damn, I wish we had a berth."

"All sold out or I would have had one," he said. He took his hand from her breasts and moved it down to her crotch. "I don't have to leave you entirely frustrated."

Meg looked at him in the dim light. Slowly she shook her head. "Oh, no . . . no, I don't think so."

He reached over and helped her hand worm through his clothes until she closed around his erection.

"Oh, God! Oh God," she whispered.

He moved his hand to her waist, then pulled up her skirt until he could get his hand under it, and slid slowly up her leg. She kissed him again and held it.

Gently he rubbed the soft spot between her legs. A moment later he could feel dampness. Then she moaned softly and bit his lip. He found the small node through the soft underwear she wore. A dozen times he caressed her until she shivered and shook and stifled a cry of rapture. She shook and shook and he held her tightly until she gave a low rumble of satisfaction.

"You did it," she whispered to him. "In a train car, for crying out loud!"

Her hand moved now, urgently. She worked his throbbing maleness out of his pants, well under his jacket, and she pumped it hard. O'Grady had felt some of her thrill at this unusual spot for lovemaking. Which it really wasn't, but close. Oh, damn he was almost there. His hips surged. His hand reached for her breasts and he rubbed them and humped again, then three more times, and he gushed with a quiet groan and pounded twice more and let out a long sigh.

Meg giggled softly. "Damn, you did it, too!"

"We did it," he said. He lay there recovering.

When she moved five minutes later, he shifted away from her and he felt her buttoning her blouse. He straightened his clothes and buttoned his pants, then shifted his coat to her.

Canyon leaned back in his own seat and tried to relax. Her head came down on his shoulder. She was still in a talkative mood.

"Whereabouts south are you going?" she asked.

"Buckeye Springs."

"Well, we'll be neighbors. I'm going to Chilesburg, which is about ten miles away." She looked over at him. "You'll be staying in the hotel there. Not very big, but adequate." She ran her fingers through his hair. "I might be able . . . That is, if you wanted, I would come and see you sometime—at the hotel."

"I'd like that. I'll be busy, but there's always time for old Irish friends to get together."

Meg laughed softly. "I like the sound of that. Get together in a real bed all bare naked and everything. I can hardly wait."

3

Meg Ryson and O'Grady arrived in St. Louis about four in the afternoon, found a hotel, and the next morning boarded a stagecoach heading for Kansas City, all the way across the state. The two-day trip covered about 180 miles and was as cramped and punishing as O'Grady had remembered stagecoaches were.

Nine people were jammed together on the three seats, with those in the middle having no back to rest against and only a strap from the coach ceiling to hold on to.

They stopped every twelve miles for fresh horses, averaged about eight miles an hour, and came to a home station every fifty miles or so for food, a quick rest stop, and again new horses. They continued right through the night, and Meg and O'Grady sagged against each other in total fatigue.

"I never want to ride in another stagecoach for as long as I live," Meg said the second morning.

In the stage station in Kansas City, O'Grady said good-bye to the beautiful young lady and she promised to see him again. O'Grady figured it was just so much talk. He walked to the Kansas City Livery and asked about his horse, Cormac. He had ridden in from Denver before he ran short of time and had to take the stage east to see the president.

Now he had a reunion with the big palomino stallion. He fed him an apple and then two lumps of sugar and brushed the pale-bronze coat and combed out the white mane and tail. The big mount rubbed his head against O'Grady in welcome.

An hour later O'Grady had Cormac saddled, and after asking for directions, he rode out of town and to the south heading for the village of Buckeye Springs.

Canyon O'Grady neared the town late in the afternoon. He passed a burned-out farm about two miles outside of town. A man stood there looking at his half-ruined barn and a house that was nothing but ashes and a brick chimney.

There was no smoke and the ashes looked to be cold. The night riders must have been at their dirty business again. O'Grady hoped that he could ride a tight line between the two factions. The "civil war" between the slavery and antislavery parties had been roaring here for three years. John Brown had done his dirty deeds and left the state. Men on both sides had been killed. The Kansas militia had been called out and federal troops from various forts had been used to help defuse the open warfare that flared from time to time.

O'Grady's reading of the current position was that the southern cause had been much the stronger in the early days of the conflict, but that now new power and emigrants from the North had edged the tide of the battle toward the antislavery population.

He was going to do his best to investigate the murder of U.S. Marshal J. B. Tippit and try to steer clear of everything else. At least that was his fondest hope. He knew the slavery question was one absolutely loaded with emotion. Normally rational men and women went crazy when the slavery question came up, and that usually led to violence.

O'Grady rode Cormac down the main street of the town and saw where a business had been burned to the ground. There was no new construction going on here as he had seen in much of the West. It was said that no thinking man would bring a wife and family into the hotbed of violence that Kansas had become.

Still, new families of the southern persuasion did come across the border from Missouri. Those coming into the territory favoring the North and antislavery had to skirt to the north of Missouri and come through Iowa and Nebraska. This route was the only one possible if a northern sympathizer wanted to bring in any weapons.

O'Grady found that Meg Ryson had been right: Buckeye Springs had only one hotel, a two-story affair almost in the middle of the small town. He guessed there were no more than five hundred people in the settlement, but many more than that in outlying sections, where some farming was starting and cattle were being raised.

The special agent for the President of the United States tied up outside the hotel, untied the carpetbag off the back of Cormac, and went in to register.

His room on the second floor was about what he expected—stark, clean, and almost bare. A bed, a dresser with a mirror, a pitcher of water and a bowl, and one chair were its only comforts. He dropped his carpetbag on the bed and went to put Cormac in the livery stable.

The stable was smaller than he had expected. Not many travelers passed through Buckeye Springs, and most of the people kept their own horses in town or on the farms and ranches.

For twenty cents a day he got a stall and some hay, but he had to furnish his own grain. He paid another nickel a day for oats and unsaddled the big palomino and brushed him down. Cormac turned and nuzzled O'Grady and rolled his big brown eyes, but there was no apple in his owner's pocket this time.

"Next time, lad," O'Grady said. "Next time it'll be an apple and sugar." On his way back to the hotel, he passed the small, wood-framed Ashland County courthouse. A sign over a side door said, SHERIFF'S DEPARTMENT.

O'Grady hesitated. He didn't know whom to trust

in this town, not with the slavery fight. He'd heard that in one east Kansas county the sheriff, judges, and the district attorney all lined up on one side of the slavery issue and wouldn't prosecute any crimes, including murders and arson, committed by men working for their side.

First he'd look around and do some careful questioning. After it got dark, he would go see the woman who wrote the first letter to the U.S. marshal's office, Tabitha Rothmore. He might try the back door of the general store just before she closed up.

O'Grady was almost back to the hotel when he saw someone riding into town. The man sat hunched over in the saddle, favoring his right shoulder. The horse moved at a slow walk, and with each step of the mount, the rider winced. He angled toward the side of the street where O'Grady stood. When the horse came to the tie rail, it stopped. The man looked at the building in front of him. O'Grady did, too, and saw that it was a doctor's office.

The rider slipped halfway out of the saddle.

O'Grady rushed out and caught him, saw the blood on his shoulder, and eased him down from the mount. The big agent put the rider's good arm over his shoulder and his arm around the man's waist and almost carried him to the boardwalk and up to the doctor's door.

"Figure you want to see the doc," O'Grady said.

"Right," the man said through tightly held lips.

Inside the doctor's office, they found a woman in a white dress who saw the blood and hurried them through a waiting area to a small room with a chair and a waist-high table. O'Grady helped the man onto the table and pushed a small pillow under his head.

A few seconds later a short, thin man with deep-set eyes and hair cut short in the Prussian style hurried into the room.

"Blinman!" The little medico shook his head. "Told you that was fire you was playing with. Told you it was gonna burn you sooner or later. Hell, the issue is nearly settled. Let it lay.''

He used some scissors to cut off a patch of the man's shirt and examined the wound.

"They didn't figure to miss, did they? You got powder burns on your shirt and skin around that bullet hole. How far away was the bastard?''

"About three feet, Doc. Can you get the slug out?''

"Sure. How loud can you scream?''

"Loud enough. Start digging. Damn thing's been in there since last night.''

"Want your friend here to help hold you down?'' the doctor asked.

"Don't know the gent.'' Blinman looked up. "Thanks, stranger. I might still be lying out there in the dust if you hadn't helped. This ain't exactly a friendly town, not anymore.''

O'Grady touched his hat and walked out of the room and the office.

He stopped by at the first saloon he saw, the Hell Hole. O'Grady snorted. Probably a well-founded name. But the best saloon in a community usually is the quickest place to find out what's going on in a town. He pushed inside, bought a beer for a dime at the bar, and settled down at the end of the polished wood to listen and wash down the trail dust at the same time.

Five minutes later a man who dressed like a clerk in a store came in and looked behind him. He asked for a beer and then talked to the apron.

"You hear that Blinman got himself shot? Last night sometime. Them night riders burned him out slicker than a whistle. Shot him on purpose, from what I hear. Punishment. A damned clear warning.''

"Which side he on?'' the barkeep asked.

"Damned if I know. But if he got shot up close that way, he must have been a northerner. I hear the southern night riders burn and then shoot the victim that way as a lesson.''

"I don't take sides," the barkeep said, holding up both hands. "Hell, I want to stay alive. I just don't take sides."

"Not that much going on anymore, Amos. You should have been here three years ago. Damn, it was hell on wheels around here in fifty-five and fifty-six. Calmed down ever so much since them wild years."

"Still, we had that hanging about two months ago."

The clerk sipped his beer, then scratched his head. "Ain't nobody thinks that had much to do with the slavery question. Far as anybody can tell, that is. That killing certainly was an interesting one."

The clerk finished his beer, nodded at the apron, and headed out the front door.

O'Grady followed him. It was getting on toward dusk. He walked the town, one end to the other, covering both sides of the street. Not a lot of town to look over. He found the general store and saw that it had the CLOSED sign out. He went to the alley and up to the back door of the store and knocked. He knocked a second and then a third time.

"Yes, who is it?" a muffled voice came from inside.

"I'm new in town, miss. I need to talk with you."

"I'm closed. Go away."

"Can't do that. I want to talk about your father."

He heard a bolt thrown, then the door edged open an inch. It was light inside.

"You said you want to talk about my father. What about?"

"I'm trying to find out who killed him."

The door came open more and he saw her. She was tiny, maybe five feet tall and eighty-five pounds wet. She had light-blond hair to her shoulders with straight bangs in front. In the lamplight he could see a strong chin and high cheekbones. She was a pretty girl—not a beauty, but pretty.

Canyon had a first impression that this girl was strong-willed and still angry.

She stared at him from soft-green eyes. "I don't see no badge. Who are you?"

"My name in Canyon O'Grady and I'm interested in your father's death and the death of the U.S. marshal who came here at the urging of your letters."

"Oh. If you know about them, then you must be a lawman. I guess it's all right to let you come in." She held open the door.

Just then a gunshot sounded behind them and a round thunked into the wood over the door.

"Don't neither of you move a tad or you're dead. Understand?" a soft southern voice called out before the sound of the shot could die out.

O'Grady froze, his hand starting down his right side.

"Yep, understand," O'Grady said.

"Good. You, big man. Move to the side and stretch your hands to the top of the door. Do it slow. I don't aim to kill nobody. Just want to relieve the little lady of her cash. She took in a basket of money today. I been watching."

The voice was still well behind them.

"Little lady, you just best unbutton your blouse there and show me what you're hiding underneath. Yeah, good idea. Do it right now."

"No!"

"What the hell you say? I got a gun."

O'Grady could see just the edge of Tabitha where she stood in the doorway. A fraction of a second later she darted to one side and was gone. The light inside blew out and the gunman roared in anger and stormed toward the door.

O'Grady timed it by the sound of the man's angry breathing. Just as he came beside the tall agent, O'Grady slammed his fist downward into the gunman's way. His fist hit the robber's right wrist, spinning his iron out of his hand. O'Grady whirled and kicked the man's legs out from under him, sprawling the man in the dust.

A split second later O'Grady pushed his big .45 under the robber's chin and pressed upward so hard it made the man cry out in pain.

"The fight is gone out of him, Miss Rothmore," O'Grady said. "Our friend is ready to apologize and swear that he's heading out of town right now."

A light bloomed in the back room of the hardware store and Tabitha carried it forward, a shotgun now under one arm. O'Grady saw that both hammers were cocked on the double barrels.

She stood looking down at the gunman lying in the dust by the back door of the hardware.

"Know him?" O'Grady asked.

"Never seen him before . . . No, I have. I sold him a box of percussion caps and linen-wrapped cartridges for a .44-caliber revolver this afternoon."

"Want me to call the sheriff?" O'Grady asked.

"Wouldn't do much good. We haven't had a trial here in the county for almost two years. Our judge quit, the district attorney was shot dead, and the sheriff is more worried about his job and his outside interests than he is in law and order."

"Stand up," O'Grady ordered the robber. The man stood slowly, O'Grady's .44 army percussion Colt never leaving his chin. "You have any money?" O'Grady asked.

"Three dollars," the man said.

"You better use that to get yourself as far out of town as you can. I'm gonna be around for a couple of weeks. I see your face anywhere, I'm gonna blow it full of extra holes. You understand?"

"Yes, sir. Do I get my six-gun back?"

"Not a chance," Tabitha said quickly. "I'm making a collection of guns men have used to try to rob me. So far I've got two. Now I'll have one more. Just for your information, nobody has robbed me yet. I've got one scalp on my scalp pole, courtesy of my trusty shotgun. You want to try again?"

The man shook his head.

O'Grady prodded him in the belly with the six-gun.

"Get out of here," he said. "All the way out of the county. Out of the territory would be safest for you."

The man turned and stared at them a minute in the light. O'Grady put a hot lead slug into the ground between his boots. He raced down the alley into the darkness.

O'Grady holstered his iron and tipped his hat.

"Now, Miss Rothmore, I need to have a confidential talk with you about your father's death and just what the U.S. marshal said and did while he was here."

Tabitha Rothmore let a small smile creep onto her pretty face. "So, I figured you had to be some kind of a lawman. Nobody else has been interested in that marshal. Come in, and we'll shut the door. That owl-hoot might just have a second iron in his saddlebag down the alley."

4

O'Grady stepped into the back room of the general store and Tabitha Rothmore quickly bolted the door and snapped a night lock. Only then did she lower the shotgun.

"Thanks for the help out there, but none was really needed. I've been fending for myself with men and boys for several years now."

O'Grady watched her in the faint lamplight and nodded. "I'll just bet that you have. Now I do need to talk to you about your father and the marshal. Nobody knows that I'm in town or why I'm here. I want to keep it that way. First, was your father taking either side in the slavery issue?"

"No, absolutely not, and neither do I. The whole thing has gotten out of hand. I wish we'd have the vote and get it over with one way or the other."

"I have a feeling even a vote won't solve the problem. It's much larger than just Kansas. The whole nation is caught up in this struggle. There's been some talk in the South of leaving the union and starting a separate country."

"That will never happen. The South is all rural and farms. They don't have mills and factories. It just wouldn't work. They will be smart enough to see that."

"Let's hope," O'Grady said. "Now, tell me about your father. If he wasn't involved in the slavery issue, who were his enemies? He must have had at least one who was angry enough to hang him."

Tabitha's pretty face shriveled into a frown.

"I've thought about that. I've stayed up all night trying to figure it out. My dad was a good man. He paid his bills, he voted, he was faithful to his wife until the day she died, he went to church every Sunday, and he had more than twenty accounts for people in town he knew would never be able to pay him. Most of them were widows or old men who had no income. I just can't figure out who would hate my father enough to . . . to kill him."

She motioned to him and they went to the side of the back-room area of the store. A small office had been set up there with a desk, some boxes for files, and a table lamp and two chairs.

"I was about to make some tea. Do you want some?"

"Yes, that would be fine." Canyon hesitated. "Miss Rothmore, what about money? Did your father owe anyone a large sum that he tried to collect, or did someone owe your father?"

"Money . . . " She frowned again as she put tea on a small cast-iron stove at the side of the room. It was used mainly to heat the back-room area, but also worked well for light cooking. Tabitha lit a fire that had been set in the firebox and put a teakettle of water on to boil.

"Money might have something to do with it. I heard Father arguing about money one night at home. I was upstairs in my room and a man came into the living room below. I didn't know who it was and Father never said. But money was the problem. Now that you mention it, that last argument was the night he was killed."

"Did your father keep books?"

"Yes, he sure did. He was an accountant at one time, so he kept excellent books. Every penny that came in and went out was down in black and white."

"Did you check over the books to hunt for any cause of the problem?"

Tabitha looked at him. "No, I haven't. It didn't occur to me, but I will. I'm still not sure just who you are, Mr. O'Grady, so I don't know why you're investigating. Are you some kind of a detective?"

Canyon O'Grady hesitated. If he couldn't trust this lady, whom could he trust.

"Miss Rothmore—"

She held up her hand stopping him. "Please, call me Tabitha."

"Yes, fine, and you call me Canyon. So, Tabitha, I'm here partly because you have a U.S. post-office station in your store. When your father was killed, it became government business. Then too, a U.S. marshal was killed investigating, so two branches of the government are concerned. They talked to the president."

Tabitha's soft-green eyes went wide. "The president? President Buchanan in Washington, D.C., knows about my father?"

"He most certainly does. I'm here to try to find out what happened and set it straight. I'm a special agent working directly under orders of President Buchanan."

"For land sakes! Now isn't that something. President Buchanan himself." Her wide-eyed surprise was soon replaced with a more practical look of concern. "Then the president must have given you a letter or some identification or something."

Canyon O'Grady took a card from his inside pocket. It was now in a soft leather case to protect it. The card itself had a tintype picture of O'Grady on it and a short printed statement that he was a representative of the United States government and should be afforded all rights and privileges of such an agent. The card was signed by James Buchanan, President. The card itself was sealed together with nearly clear isinglass on both sides. He showed it to the girl. She read it and her soft-green eyes widened again.

"I swear I won't tell anybody who you are or why you're here. Golly! President Buchanan himself."

"Four days ago I was fishing with the president along a mountain stream in New England," O'Grady said. "He caught the biggest fish, then we ate them for dinner."

Tabitha worked with the fire, then the teakettle and at last brought tea to him where he sat beside the desk.

He thanked her for the brew, added some sugar, and then sipped it.

"Good," he said. "Now, what do you think about the books? Would you help me look through them? There might be something that would give us a quick start in finding your father's killer. Once we know who that is, we'll be able to tie down who killed the marshal as well."

"Oh, that's the easy part," Tabitha said. "Torris Canatale killed the marshal in a shootout in the saloon. Everyone knows that."

O'Grady nodded. "Yes, right, and I'll follow up on that. So first let's work on who killed your father."

She opened a drawer and took out three account books. They were bound single-edge ledgers and showed daily receipts of the Buckeye Springs General Store. On another page was a month-by-month list of expenses, showing payments made to wholesale houses, some locals, including the blacksmith, and a harness maker.

O'Grady concentrated on the expense listings from a year ago. He found the usual items, then toward the end of each month there was a thirty-dollar listing for "night watchman for month."

O'Grady stared at the entry, checked for several months, and found the same entry. Then, at the first of 1857, the night watchman got a raise to sixty dollars a month. That seemed a little high. Two dollars a day for a night watchman. He looked at the entries for the two months before Stanley Rothmore died and found no entries at all for night watchman.

He showed Tabitha the items. "Do you remember

who the night watchman was for the store?'' O'Grady asked.

''Must be some mistake. We've never had a watchman. Pa said it was a waste of money in a place like Buckeye Springs.''

''Then why the thirty- and then sixty-dollar monthly fees paid to a night watchman?''

Tabitha looked at him with puzzlement. ''I honestly don't know. But for certain there never has been a hired night watchman at this store in the past three years.''

O'Grady rubbed his chin and stared at the entries. ''Did your father use bank drafts to send payments to people? Some people are calling them checks. Did he have a checkbook?''

''Of course. We paid the wholesalers in Chicago and St. Louis with bank drafts. He had a whole book of them printed. I still use them the same way.''

''And each of the drafts has a stub showing the amount and to whom the amount was paid?''

''Yes, of course.''

''Good. Where are your stubs for last year?''

They looked through a box under a counter and found them. O'Grady located the right month and then looked for the date the night watchman had been paid. There was no record in any of the stubs about a night watchman's salary and no amount of thirty or sixty dollars.

''Told you so,'' the girl said.

''So, where did the thirty dollars and then the sixty dollars a month go? It was paid out by your father to someone. It must have been paid in cash—so it couldn't be traced.''

''Maybe that was what my pa was arguing about with that man I heard the night he died.'' She looked at the monthly listings. ''Yes, look. There are no entries for the three months before Pa died for night watchman. Maybe he had quit paying this man, and he got mad and—''

"Hang your employer when he fires you?" O'Grady asked. "Doesn't seem reasonable." Then the agent remembered something else. "In some of the big cities there are protection rackets. Where hoodlums get protection money from merchants so the store won't get its windows smashed and merchandise destroyed. Could there be something like that going on here in Buckeye Springs?"

Tabitha shrugged. "I really don't know. I guess it could. But since Pa has died, no one has approached me about that." She scowled. "I guess if that's why Pa got killed the same man wouldn't want to come back and pressure me. He might think I knew more about it than I do."

"I'll check with some of the other merchants in town. That won't be hard to figure out. It just might be a small clue to why your pa died. Now, it's getting late. I'll walk you home and then get some sleep myself. I'm going to have a busy day tomorrow. Remember, you don't even know who I am. I'll be telling everyone that I'm here to look for a business to buy or to start a new one. That will let me ask a lot of questions."

Tabitha reached for a shawl and carried the lamp toward the back door. "You really don't need to walk home with me. I'll be fine."

"But that man we scared off might come back and follow you."

Tabitha carried a package over her arm. She flipped it aside and O'Grady found himself staring at a small-caliber revolver muzzle. He saw four rounds in the five-shot cylinder.

"I've only had to use it once, but by now most of the men in town know I carry it. I never have any trouble."

"Just the same, I'll feel better," O'Grady said.

He walked her the two blocks to her two-story house and waited until she was inside and had a lamp lit and the door locked. Then O'Grady hurried back to his

41

hotel room and went to sleep the moment his head hit the pillow.

Exactly at midnight, eight men met at the old ice-house out at the edge of town near Fifth Street. The icehouse was nearly empty this late in the year, with only a few more chunks of ice resting under their insulation blankets of straw.

Jim Washington greeted each man quietly as he rode up. He made sure each had a rifle and a revolver and that all were properly loaded. When they all were there, they faded away from the icehouse one at a time and met again in the moonlight a mile north of town near the creek.

Washington gathered them around him. Kinole was there and Carter, this time on a dun, and the five others they had ridden with now for almost two years.

"Men, tonight we go see Diego Nickler. He's got a small cattle operation about four more miles north. We'll torch his barn and two sheds, and when he and his woman and kids leave the house, we'll be coming up behind and set it on fire. Any questions?"

"I hear the pro-slavery assholes been close up shooting the men in the right arm," Kinole said. "Happened last night to Blinman, the farmer south of town. We gonna return the compliment with Nickler?"

Washington waited a minute to let the men talk it up. Most of them were in favor of the idea. "All right, we'll do one of the men, if we can catch him easy. I don't want nobody getting hot tonight over a damn barn. Now, let's ride. We got about four more miles to his ranch. We come in quiet. We got the coal oil?"

Two men said they each had two one-gallon tins. The night riders pounded down the north road.

Washington stopped the riders a quarter of a mile from the barn. He had brought them around the other farm buildings so they could ride in from the north at the barns. There were two of them.

They walked their mounts the last three hundred yards. Then Washington picked two men to go into each barn on foot and set them afire. They always started hay burning if they could find any. It started easy and was impossible to put out.

Washington sat on his horse watching. If it went as usual, the four men would be back well before the fires broke out in the open where the ranch workers could see them. By that time they would be firing the two sheds and the bunkhouse. He was always certain to start the fire at the far end of the bunkhouse so the men were not trapped inside.

He watched now as flames gushed from the first barn through a large open back door. The rancher couldn't see it yet.

Two men ran back, excitement wreathing their faces.

"Got ours burning good," Carter said as he mounted his horse and waited.

The other two came back a minute later and Washington moved them around to where the sheds and the bunkhouse were. He sent different men in to these targets and told them when they were done to find their horses and circle to the south below the ranch house.

As soon as the four men headed for the three buildings, Washington led his three men and himself on a circular ride around the bunkhouse and the big house and to the south. They tied their horses in the fringes of brush along the creek and took the last two cans of coal oil and walked cautiously toward the dark ranch house.

"Fire," a voice bellowed from the ranch yard. Flames spurted out a front man-size door of the barn.

Lights blinked on in the ranch house. Washington could see men sprinting for the well house and grabbing buckets. Now flames billowed out of both the barns. Horses screamed in the adjoining corral and one of the hands opened the gate and hoorahed the animals to safety.

More lights burned in the big house and the back screen door slammed. A heavier voice roared out some questions and the men formed a bucket brigade, but both barns were completely in flames and couldn't be touched.

Then fire broke out in the wagon shed and the bunkhouse. That was the time to move. Washington led the attack on the farmhouse. It was a three-story affair with about ten rooms. They sloshed kerosene in one bedroom window and dropped a burning newspaper on it. The other can of oil they poured over the front door and lit it and then raced away.

"Hold it," a heavy voice snarled.

The night riders kept running. A shotgun blasted and James Washington bellowed in pain as some of the scattered buckshot drove into his legs. He lifted his drawn pistol and fired five times at the shotgunner.

The man with the shotgun took the first .44 round in the leg and doubled over. The next two hit him in the shoulder, and when he lifted up, the fourth round hit him in the heart and threw him backward into the suddenness of death.

Washington and his men ran back to their horses.

"I'm hit with buckshot," one of the men brayed.

"So am I," Washington snapped. "You ain't dead, and neither am I, so keep running. We'll patch you up when we get back to town."

Before they found their horses, they heard hoofbeats coming toward them. Some of the cowboys were giving chase.

"Down," Washington ordered. We'll form a V toward the ranch and blast the bastards if they get close enough."

The four men waited. The ranch riders came closer.

"Can't be our men," Washington said. "They wouldn't ride that fast and make that much noise."

The night riders waited again. Soon they could see three riders coming toward them, all waving rifles, yelling back and forth.

"Over this way," one yelled. "They killed Nickler in cold blood. Let's ride down the bastards."

The riders were going to miss the V. One of Washington's men aimed at the voices and fired his rifle. The three ranch men changed direction and charged at the spot, firing rifles as they came.

The men on the ground had the advantage. They could hear and soon see their targets. The riders saw only blobs ahead in the plains.

"Wait until you get here," Washington told his closely spaced men. This time they waited. When the riders were within thirty feet of the four men lying on the ground, Washington's men began firing.

Two of the riders slammed out of their saddles grievously wounded. The third took two slugs in the arm and shoulder, fell over his horse's neck, and the animal raced back toward the ranch house.

When the horses were gone, Washington lifted up. "Anybody hit?" he asked.

"I got a nick in the leg," one man said.

"Fine. Let's find our horses and the other four men and get back to town. How is the man hit with buckshot?"

"I'm doing great. Guess I didn't pick up more than four or five of the shot.

It took them a half-hour to find the other four riders, then they moved back to town, in twos, coming in from different directions and riding into town and slipping into Washington's house.

Washington washed out the buckshot wounds and treated the man's leg nicked by the rifle. Then they all had a drink of sippin whiskey and three went home.

"We did a good night's work, men," Washington told them.

"Yeah, Carter said, "but we probably killed three men."

"This is the Kansas Civil War, Carter. Hell of a lot better we kill some damn slave-lover than one of us gets killed."

The last three had one more drink to that and went home.

5

The next morning talk around town was about the killings and burning out at the Diego Nickler ranch and how he and two of his hands had been shot to death and all the buildings burned to the ground. Nickler was well-known in town as a pro-slavery advocate.

Over breakfast O'Grady asked the owner about a protection racket. The small-café owner merely shrugged. He had a white apron around his middle and his hair slicked back to keep it out of the food.

"Don't know what the hell you talking about. Anybody tries to shake any money out of my tree gets a face full of forty-four hot lead."

"That's a good way to handle the situation. Oh, I'd prefer that you don't say anything about this. It's a small investigation I'm doing that has to be very hush-hush."

The café man nodded. "Fine by me. How did you like the ham and eggs?"

"They were fine, and those grated and fried potatoes were the best I've had."

"Good, come back for noon and then supper. I serve a good Kansas grain-fed steak."

O'Grady finished his meal, left the café, and went to the next store, a small hardware and tin-goods dealer. The store-owner listened to O'Grady and then kicked the counter.

"Yeah, some half-brain talked to me about protection. I told him that a dollar a day was about what I cleared after I paid the rent. I led him to the door and threw his ass right out onto the street in the dirt and cow pies. He never come back.''

''I think that's a good way to handle these ruffians,'' O'Grady said. He went to the next place, a small jewelry shop.

O'Grady used his looking-to-buy-a-business line and got a reaction from the jeweler, Kinole.

''I sure never would start a business in this territory again if I was to do it over. Business ain't good. Not in this town, not in Kansas. Mostly people fight here. You must have heard about the North and the South fight. Some folks call this the Kansas 'civil war'. My advice: start a business in Nebraska or Iowa or Missouri. Not here. Been three businesses burned out so far, mostly by pro-slavery farmers hereabouts.''

''Can't you get protection? An association, a service of some kind?''

''Oh, hell, we got that, but it ain't really protection. It's nothing but a small-time racket he's working on the side.''

''Who is working a racket? Who should I watch out for if I do start up here?''

Kinole looked at him hard, then shook his head. ''Nope, don't want to get in trouble. I didn't join this little service for two months. Second month I got a brick through my plate-glass window. Cost me thirty dollars for a new one. I signed up the next day. I shouldn't even be talking about it. Now, if you ain't buying anything, I got a timepiece to repair.''

O'Grady thanked him, left, and checked three more stores. Two of the merchants claimed they didn't have time to talk. They were obviously afraid to discuss the subject. The third store was a saddlery. The man pulled a knife through leather and shook his head. He was a bull of a man with large, powerful shoulders, heavy jowls, sagging eyebrows, a florid face, and a stiff, full mustache. His hair was wild and only partly combed.

The man's hands were large, strong, and wielded the knife like a surgeon.

He wore range pants, a checkered shirt open halfway to his waist. In the early fall day he wiped sweat off his face and looked at O'Grady.

"Ain't had no trouble with them protection guys since I whupped that yahoo's ass one day. He come sniffing around saying how it was so dangerous with the slavery and antislavery people shooting up the town. I told the young no-good that I was from Texas and I'd seen every kind of protection racket going. I wasn't about to fall for his.

"I turned around and grabbed my sawed-off shotgun and put a round just over his head into the wall, right up there. Then I dropped my aim, the second barrel pointing dead on his belly, and he took off so fast he damn near left his shoes in the store. Ain't heard nothing from him since."

The saddle maker positioned a blank piece of leather on his bench and put a saddle-skirt pattern over it, tracing it with an awl.

"Advice to you, young man is to shoot first. If'n you 'light here and open a store, give that gent the bum's rush when he comes in and talks about merchant protection. Now, I had my say and you're warned."

O'Grady thanked him and moved down the street. He worked ten more stores, and found only one owner who would admit that he was paying a protection service to watch his store.

No one had even hinted at a name. "No-good," was as close as he had for a name. Who was this person? As he thought about it, O'Grady walked back to the general store and looked at the overhang. Near the end was where Stanley Rothmore had been hanged. The beam was open and ten feet off the ground.

How would you get a man hoisted that high? How would you get a rope over the beam? A man standing on a horse could reach it. Maybe they had Rothmore sitting backward on a horse in the best lynching style.

Maybe. They? Yes, it would have taken more than one man to do the whole thing: place the rope with the noose over the beam, get Rothmore on a horse, put the noose around his neck, pull it tight, and tie it off. More than one killer.

So, he was making progress. Now, if the damned Kansas civil war would ease off so he could find the killer.

Almost as he thought it, Canyon heard shots from a block away. Then someone far off screamed, "Fire." The word was picked up and repeated down the block as half a dozen men ran to the north and down the first cross street off Main. O'Grady ran with them.

The burning house was another block away. Already a solid column of back and gray smoke surged skyward. As he ran closer, O'Grady could see fire coming out the upstairs windows of the two-story frame house.

Not even a Washington, D.C., fire department could save this house.

O'Grady got as close as he could, but half a dozen men surged back from the heat, the water in their buckets unthrown.

"Too damn hot," one of them shouted.

"Anybody inside?" a voice asked.

Off to one side a man screamed. He lay behind a picket fence in the next yard. He was tied hand and foot and had chewed through a gag.

"It's Bruce Deatherage," someone shouted. "That's his house burning."

A man untied Deatherage and he stood crying as his house burned to the ground. His wife and two small sons had been tied up and dumped over the fence as well. They huddled together as the flames ate up everything they owned.

"The damned pro-slavers done it," Deatherage screamed. "I saw them. I recognized one of them when his mask slipped. Three of them rode up to my back door asking directions. The one I damn well recognized was Elroy Smithson, that rancher out south of town. It was him, all right. Soon as I can borrow a rifle, I'm going out there and shoot him dead."

"Tit for tat," a man standing near O'Grady said to no one in particular.

"How's that?" O'Grady asked the man.

"Last night the antislavery people burned out Diego Nickler, killed him and two of his hands. Now, today, Bruce Deatherage gets his house burned up. Tit for tat. Now it looks like it's the turn for the antislavery forces to strike."

"I'm a stranger in town," O'Grady said. "Somebody told me that the election is coming up and the antislavery group is bound to win. Isn't the fighting about over?"

"Can't tell it around here. The pro-slavers will battle right down until the ballots are counted." The man shook his head. "Don't count on them to stop fighting even then. If I don't miss my guess, Kansas is in for another five years of fire and rifle and lots of troubles."

O'Grady walked over where the burned-out family stood.

"Bruce, you and the family are gonna stay at our house tonight. Then tomorrow we'll start putting together some clothes and furniture for you." The man talking was a neighbor from nearby. He led the family across the dusty street to his house as the last wall of the house fell in with a shower of sparks and smoke.

O'Grady headed back for Main Street. Someone fell into step next to him. He looked over, to find Tabitha Rothmore walking beside him. It was a pleasant change from the stark reality of an arson fire and a family reduced to abject poverty.

"More trouble," Tabitha said. "Sometimes I wish these arsonists and killers would all move to Arizona or California or somewhere, just so they leave Kansas. They're killing our chances to become a state. I really believe that."

They walked along for fifty feet without talking.

"Did you see the look on that poor woman's face when

she held her two little boys? She was frantic. She'll have nightmares about today for a long, long time.''

"The way you still do?'' O'Grady asked.

She looked up quickly at him, her blond hair swinging as she turned. Soft-green eyes clouded slightly, then she nodded. "Yes, exactly, the way I still do. I'll have them until the men who killed Daddy are behind bars or dead themselves. I'll be glad to pull the trigger on them if it comes to that. Lord knows there won't be a trial. Hasn't been a court case come to trial in this county in over two years now.''

"That long?''

"True. One judge quit, another got run out of town, and the judge drawing his pay now is a drunk who used to be a barkeep at one of the saloons in the next town. His friend the territorial governor appointed him judge.''

"Sorry to hear that, which means that if we're wanting any justice here, we're not talking about arresting the men who killed your father.''

"Wouldn't do any good. The sheriff would probably let them out of jail the next day.''

"I am making some progress. I talked to at least two of the merchants who are paying protection money, but neither one would say who they paid.''

"Which doesn't help us much.'' She stopped and watched him closely. "The more I think about it, the more I'm feeling that maybe Daddy's death must be a part of this slavery problem. He never talked a lot about it, but he must have said something one way or the other that made somebody mad.''

"Then why didn't they burn down his store?'' O'Grady asked. "No, I think it was something different. It very well could be the protection racket.''

"So how do we prove it?''

"I don't know. And now, with the night riders striking right in the middle of the day this way, it's going to make it harder than ever to get people thinking about your father's death.''

He saw her face work and nearly dissolve into tears. Then she bit her lower lip, brushed her eyes with the back of her hand. "I still can't belive that he's gone. If he'd been sick or lingered awhile, I would have had time to get used to the idea. The way it happened was a total shock."

"Death is always brutal, but that way it's twice as bad." He walked beside her. "Do you remember anything more about the voices you heard downstairs the night before? Was it a man's voice or a woman's?"

"Oh, a man's voice."

"A higher voice or a low voice?"

"Lower, like he would sing bass."

"That helps a little. I'm out of ideas from this side. I want to work the marshal's death and see what I can get there. Something might tie in with your father."

They were at the store. She unlocked the front door and waved him inside. "Could you come in a minute? I want to talk a little more."

He nodded and went inside.

Tabitha went to the back and took off the light jacket the dress had with it. Straps came over her shoulders and the form-fitting dress outlined her figure well. She walked to the door that led into the back room and motioned to him.

"I come back here sometimes when there's no one out front. I know I can run the store, but I still want to know for sure why Father died and who killed him. Is that asking too much?"

"No, not too much at all."

Tabitha stepped near him, stretched up, caught his face with her hands, and pulled it down so she could kiss his lips. She held it for a moment, then let him go. She pushed against him and her arms went around his back.

"Canyon O'Grady, I've been wanting to do that since the first time I saw you." She leaned back and looked up at him. "I hope you don't think I'm too forward."

He laughed softly. "Young lady, not at all. I like a woman who knows what she's interested in and isn't too bashful to admit it. Makes things a lot easier if nobody is bluffing and posturing and saying things they don't mean."

He bent and put his arms around her waist and lifted her feet off the floor until her face was even with his. "My turn," he said, and kissed her lips gently, then more insistently. She returned the pressure and let her mouth edge open a moment, then closed it. She pushed her breasts hard against his chest, and when he ended the kiss, she sighed softly and dropped her head to his shoulder.

"Damn! Right now I wish I was this tall all the time, then I could kiss you easier."

She grinned and they both laughed. He was about to kiss her again when the small bell over the front door rang as someone came in.

"Oh, damn," Tabitha said.

"Ladies shouldn't swear," O'Grady said. He pecked a kiss on her lips and put her back on the floor.

"O'Grady, that was fine. I swear because I'm no lady. I hope we can get back to the kissing part one of these days."

"Too much foot traffic around here." He kissed her lips gently again, turned her, and aimed her at the door to the store. "Besides, I have to go out there and find a killer."

Tabitha grinned, blew him a kiss, and hurried into the front of the store.

O'Grady went out the back door, down the alley to the cross street and up to Main. He had to find out where Torris Canatale lived or worked or which saloon he spent time in. That might take some time. Then, if he could locate the man, he would follow him and try to establish some kind of a pattern. He hoped it would be a pattern that would help explain the death of Marshal Tippit.

6

"Goddamnit, I'm not sure! I'm not positive he saw me when my mask slipped down. That's the hell of it. He sure as shit could have. Do I take off for the next county or turn my ranch into an armed and fortified camp? Christ! It was all going fine, then he looked up just as that brat of his grabbed my kerchief and pulled it down."

Elroy Smithson slammed the flat of his hand down on the kitchen table in the ranch house on the Flying S Ranch eight miles south of Buckeye Springs. He and two men had just ridden in after the morning outing to town with cans of coal oil.

"Man, did that house burn," Guy Emmons said as he pulled at a bottle of beer. "Don't think I ever saw a two-story six-room house go up in smoke so fast."

"Green lumber," the other man at the table said. He was Del Ziegler, a hand on the ranch and a member of the pro-slavery night riders. "Damn, I could smell the pitch coming out of them boards as they started to burn like a prairie fire."

"Shut up, both of you! I've got a problem here. Del, you take some food and ride north a mile to that little clump of trees and you be lookout. You see more than one rider coming this way from town, you get your butt back in here so fast you'll cause a trail of smoke. We don't want to be surprised."

"Hell, who's gonna come?" Guy asked. "Damn sheriff won't get his tail out of his office. He's the only law around here."

"I'm thinking of the antislavery night riders, you fart stopper," Smithson said. "I damn well should have shot that prick Deatherage right then. Don't know why I didn't."

"His old lady was watching you, that's why," Guy said. "We didn't know the guy was gonna see your face."

Smithson stared at Del. "Don't just stand there, peckerhead. Get some food and get out of here. Some of them crazy northerners might be on the way right now. We'll damn well stand guard tonight around the barns and ranch house."

Smithson scowled as he tipped his warm bottle of beer. He was an average-size man, five-nine, with 150 pounds on his loose jointed frame. He could ride a horse all day and never feel tired. He had a flat face and almost no bridge to his nose between eyes so light blue they almost looked white. The bright sun bothered his eyes and they watered all summer.

He scraped one hand back through his thinning hair. It had been brown, and what was left struggled to cover his scalp. He had slender, hairy arms and hair sticking out from the V in his shirt. He buttoned and then unbuttoned the natural-color leather vest and reached for the makings of a cigarette in one of the vest pockets.

"Yeah, we'll be watching tonight. The bastards have a name now, I'd bet my bundle on it. Guy, you get back on your nag and ride and call the roll. We need the other five men here tonight. Tell them it's not an official raid; we're just doing some preventive work. You got two ranches to go to, so better get moving. Have them back here before dark. You stay for supper at the Johnson ranch and ride back with Bryan."

Guy shrugged. "Guess it beats hunting strays. You didn't tell me I was gonna be a damned errand boy." He headed for the cupboards. "Can I make a couple of sandwiches first?"

Smithson waved at him, went up to his second-story

den, and looked out the window to the north. At least he didn't see any cloud of dust coming.

Maybe he was overreacting. What he had to do was set up a series of attacks, take the offensive, keep the bastards off-balance. He had two more targets; then he'd burn down the damn newspaper, it was 90 percent antislavery. He had his orders, and he damn well would carry them out.

If he did his job well enough, Kansas would vote pro-slavery, pro-South, and he would be in line for one of the U.S. senator seats from the new state of Kansas. Senator Elroy Smithson. That had a great ring to it. He hadn't been blasting and burning and rousting northerners out of the county for three years for nothing. It had to pay off. It would pay off.

They were almost there. The tide was still with them, despite all the northerners who flooded into the state. The pro-slavery party would bring in more men across the river from Missouri when the time came for the vote. Hell, they could get more than four thousand men to cross the river for one day to vote. It might cost five dollars a head, but it would pay off.

Hell, they had done it the first time to organize the territory. They had a pro-South legislature and governor. All the territorial officers were pro-South. Now they had to make it official and vote for statehood with the slavery block.

The door to his den opened and he was about to yell at whoever it was to leave him alone. Then he turned and saw Fanny standing there, wearing only those slinky silk bloomers. He grinned. Fanny had the best set of tits he'd seen in years. She had been a whore in town before he found her and brought her out here to the ranch.

He'd sent his wife and kids back to Missouri two years ago when it got brutal out here. No place to have a family, for damn sure.

"Come on in, darling. Just thinking about you."

She pranced over to him so her breasts swung and

jiggled the way he liked them to, and she pushed up against him where he sat in the chair. One breast just happened to touch his lips and his mouth opened.

"Oh, God," he said as he sucked the mound into his mouth.

"Smitty, you know how that excites me, just makes me want you. Can we get to bed early tonight?"

Smithson changed to the fresh breast. "What the fuck is the matter with right now?" He stood and caught her and eased her down to the floor on her back and ripped a hole in the bloomers where the crotch had been.

"Smitty, you do the damnedest things, but I love it."

"For what I'm paying you, Fanny, you better love it."

He pulled open his pants and didn't even take them off, lancing into her hard and fast. She screamed and howled and brayed as he slammed forward as hard as he could. He drove her up the bare wood floor and she screeched in pain as the floor burned her back.

He grunted and panted and then burst and pounded hard four more times. At once he rolled away from her and buttoned his pants. Smithson stood and looked down at her. One of her hands had snaked down to her crotch to find the small node of pleasure. She rubbed it now, evidently hardly aware that he was watching.

Smithson snorted and left the room and checked on his rifle and shotgun. He had plenty of solid cartridges for the rifle and a box of twenty-five shells for the ten-gauge shotgun, all double-ought buck.

He went to the bunkhouse. Two men were there. He told them to be on the lookout for raiders.

"Damn northerners might raid us tonight," he said. "Tell the rest of the men, and keep your weapons handy."

Two more men were working in the corral with a

new horse they were trying to break. He warned them as well.

"Where's Frisco?"

"Went to the south range to check on a downed steer," one of the hands said. "He took six men with him."

Smithson found out that Frisco, his foreman, should be back well before dark.

He stood there looking north toward the town. It was almost over. It had to be almost over. He was getting tired. The men he had recruited for the South were getting tired. He'd heard talk of secession. Damn, he'd been fighting for three years already. If the South tried to pull out of the union, it would mean fighting. That would take another three or four or five years. Damn, it could be ten years before this whole thing was over and the South and Kansas were free of the northerners.

Waddie Yaddow would be along in two days. He made a swing around the country every month to check on his captains.

Waddie was the major in charge of this section of Kansas for the pro-slavery organization. The closer to the Missouri border, the smaller the sections became because there were more people there. Waddie was paid by somebody, Smithson didn't know who for sure. He'd heard that all of the majors were really employees of the Territory of Kansas and on the territorial payroll. So the damned northerners' taxes were helping to pay for their own demise. Smithson liked that.

The whole idea was to keep the pressure on the antislavery people. They had been doing so for three years, but somehow the antislavery group seemed to be growing. If he burned out one, two more seemed to jump up to take his place.

Smithson automatically picked out where he would put his defensive men with rifles as soon as they all got back. One in the hayloft of each barn, one on the flat section of the bunkhouse roof. Two in each of the upstairs ranch-house windows. Then he wanted look-outs in place at one- and three-mile distances to the north and west.

If he was coming to attack this ranch, he'd swing all the way around and come in from the south. He made a mental note to put one more lookout a mile to the south.

Back in the kitchen, he found the cook busy with the evening meal. He was cooking for fifteen now, counting Fanny, even though she ate in her room and didn't eat much. He liked a woman with some meat on her bones and big tits, but Fanny served him just fine. When he was younger, he liked to get his dick wet once a day, but lately he'd been slowing down some.

Fanny was ready to go half a dozen times a day, but he told her to leave the crew alone or he'd chop her up in little pieces. She was his woman and nobody else's. He told her to forget she used to be a whore and keep her knees together. She tried.

Smithson went into the living room and flopped on the couch. Damn, he was tired. He tried never to do it, but now he couldn't help but think of all of the families he had burned out, of the men he had chased on horse-back, of the five or six he had whipped. Yes, a few had died. He hadn't intentionally killed anyone.

That farm family he thought was out of the house. The parents and three children burned to death in there. He hadn't meant to kill anyone, but something had to be done. Someone had to do it. He had started out as a member of a loosely knit group that guarded the trails coming into Kansas from Missouri. Anyone who was from the North was turned around and headed back. Usually they took any weapons the men carried.

Then, early in 1854, he had been approached to move down here and make a land claim and start a ranch and hold the ground for the South. They had helped him get started, even brought him two hundred head of cattle he knew had been rustled from a northerner, but he didn't care.

So he became the "captain" of the southern proponents around Buckeye Springs who wanted Kansas to vote as a slave state. He did as he was told, even innovated a few times, and was lauded by the major more than once.

From time to time, Smithson became angry with the pro-slavery people. He admitted it. He had good reason. He had been near the Pottawatomie Creek that fateful evening in May 1856 when John Brown and his band had terrorized the area.

Smithson had known James Doyle and his two sons. Even now it made him cringe and the old anger surged up.

John Brown had called himself a soldier from the "northern army," that night. He had barged into the Doyle family cabin on Mosquito Creek and told James Doyle he was under arrest and hurried him outside in the dark. A minute later they came back for the two older sons, sixteen and twenty years old.

John Brown and four of his sons and three other men pushed the three Doyles two hundred yards from the cabin and there hacked them to death with short swords. It was three brutal murders and John Brown made sure by shooting James Doyle in the head long after he was dead.

Smithson heard later what happened next. John Brown and his murderous team moved a mile on down Mosquito Creek to the Wilkinson family cabin. They lured Allen Wilkinson outside to direct them to a neighbor's house.

Only then did they ask him if he was opposed to the northern party. He said he was.

John Brown told him he was under arrest and said Wilkinson must come with them. They rushed him away without his shoes and walked him 150 yards down the road. The swords swung and Wilkinson went down, dead before he hit the ground.

The assassination squad moved on down the creek to where it entered the Pottawatomie River. There they found the James Harris cabin and quizzed him about his pro-slavery leanings. John Brown spared him, but a man in an adjoining cabin, William Sherman, was taken outside and a short way from the cabin he was hacked to death with the brutal short swords.

Smithson sat there in the living room remembering it all. Those five killings, which became known as the Pottawatomie Massacre, had enflamed the southern forces. Even now, the memory stirred anger in Smithson. It was a just cause, and if it had to be done outside the law, he would do it.

Law and order would come quickly enough once the final vote was taken and the southern pro-slavery party was firmly in control. That would mean the new state of Kansas was represented in Washington, D.C., by pro-slavery senators and representatives.

Smithson knew it had to happen. He had to keep up the work, had to keep his spirits up, and dammit, do whatever had to be done.

7

The same day that Bruce Deatherage's house burned to ashes, a ground swell of resentment surfaced in Buckeye Springs.

"Enough is enough," one of the merchants shouted. Men gathered on street corners, in the barber shop, and in saloons talking about it. This lawlessness had to stop, or they had to form their own militia to protect themselves.

That afternoon about forty men lined up outside the Hell Hole Saloon and a retired sergeant from the army tried to form them into some kind of military unit. Each man carried a rifle and a pistol. Each had a grin as if this were some kind of an adventure.

Sergeant Luke Velman looked at his recruits and laughed.

"You sons of bitches look about as much like a company of soldiers as your sisters would. Hell, I can't turn you into army overnight, but we can damn well organize and keep these southern bastards from burning down our houses and stores.

"You believe this continual warfare has gone far beyond the damn problem of slavery. We're talking just surviving here. You want to live for the next few weeks, you stick with us. I don't care if you own slaves or not, or want to own them, or would never own them. This is war, them against us. Labels don't matter a damn bit when somebody is shooting at you or throwing a burning torch at your house.

"Now, I've had my say. I've lined you up in squads,

forty men, four men per squad. The first one on the end is the corporal. Your job is to know where your other three men are at all times and be able to contact them and roust them out for duty within five minutes."

He pointed to two men he knew. "Willy and Pete, you'll be my two buck sergeants. Your job is to contact your five corporals. You divide them up however you want to.

"Reaction is our biggest job. If something happens, we got to react within five minutes or the town could go up in smoke. Sergeants divide up the corporals. Corporals learn your men's names and where they live and work and how to get in touch with them damn fast. Do this now."

O'Grady stood on the boardwalk in front of the hardware listening to the sergeant. The man was talking like a major or a colonel. He knew what had to be done and he set out to do it quickly. The man was right: this struggle had become one of survival. Right now it didn't matter if you were pro-slave or antislave, the immediate problem was to keep your house or your business from being burned to the ground.

O'Grady went into the general store and found Tabitha waiting on a customer. She pointed him to the back through the open door and he strolled back there. When she was done with the man buying nails, she hurried back, her face flushed, shoulder-length blond hair swirling around her shoulders and her soft-green eyes flashing her pleasure.

"Glad you came," she said. She put her arms around him and kissed him warmly, then nestled against his chest. "What's happening outside?"

He told her.

"Oh, dear. Now it's like a war. We have a small army and they'll have a bigger army. I might not have any future at all here. Not if they burn down the store. I have very little money in the bank account Daddy set up in Kansas City."

He held her, nuzzling into her hair. "I don't think

it'll come to an all-out war. Not yet at least. I'm making a little progress on the protection racket. I'm trying to find out who is behind it, but so far not much luck. This guy Canatale is a devious sort. Hard to find. Somebody said he spent most of his time in the saloons and the brothels.''

Tabitha held him tighter then, her breasts crushed against his chest. She reached up for another kiss, and as she probed gently into his mouth, the front bell rang.

She sighed and pulled away. "Damn," she muttered as she checked her hair, then shrugged and patted his shoulder and went out into the store.

"Yes, sir, Mr. Jordan, how can I help you today? How is that new porch coming along you're adding to your house?''

Canyon slipped out the back door of the store. He still had about twenty-five merchants to check. There were some forty stores in town and he'd covered not quite half. If someone was getting two dollars a day from thirty of them, that would be sixty dollars a day or eighteen hundred a month, and over twenty-one thousand a year. A nice little income when a store clerk earned only $360 a year. It would be an income well worth the risk of killing to protect. A merchant death would help keep the others in line, encourage those not paying to pay.

Even the death of a U.S. marshal could be risked for that kind of money. Now all O'Grady had to do was figure out who was doing it.

Elroy Smithson saw the lone rider coming toward the house just before dusk that same day. He knew it wasn't one of his riders. The man did not sit his mount well; he slouched to the side as if he had a sore butt. Smithson hurried down the stairs and to the front yard to meet the man.

His eyes lit up with anticipation when he saw the rider was Major Waddie Yaddow. The man waved and swung down from the dun. Elroy motioned to one of the hands who had come out of the bunkhouse. The man took the major's horse to the barn for some oats and water.

" 'Evening, Elroy," Waddie said.

" 'Evening, Major. I got a soft pillow and some sipping whiskey right inside where it's a mite cooler."

"Know the way to a man's butt and his soul, Captain Smithson," Yaddow said.

After the whiskey had warmed their insides, the major got down to business.

"I just rode through Buckeye Springs. The place is all riled up about your burning out that nigger-lover this morning. They've organized a watch force, a damn militia. I saw them recruit forty men, all with rifles and pistols and a crusty old ex-army sergeant who knows how to handle men and set up lookouts. He's got ten squads of four men each with ten corporals and two sergeants. He's got a damned army up there."

"You don't bring good news. I got another house and a store up there on my list."

"Forget your list, Smithson. We're gonna do the whole damn town. The sacking of Lawrence won't even be remembered by the time we get through with Buckeye Springs."

"Fine, fine, but I've only got ten men. How do we go up against forty?"

"You don't. I've got forty men of my own coming. It's a roving force we use in hot spots, and Buckeye Springs has just qualified. The men are a half-day behind me, and they're going around Buckeye Springs."

"Forty! They got rations?"

Major Yaddow looked up sharply. "Some rations. We'll be bunking ten at the other three ranches we control nearby. I wouldn't dump forty hungry men on you. Now, let's settle down and do some important planning. I'll need to know which way the wind blows so we'll know where to start the first building on fire.

"If we get one of those big wooden store buildings

burning good, it'll take out a whole block. They're pasted up one against the other like match boxes."

"Easy on the wind. It always blows west to east, unless we're having a bad thunderstorm or a tornado."

"Noted. We'll give the men a day to rest up, then hit the town at three o'clock in the morning. Fewer people to deal with that way."

"I called a meeting of my eight men here tonight, including two of the ranchers. You can meet them and keep up their spirits." Smithson paused and stared at the major. "Just how the hell are we doing? I hear all sorts of things. In town they're saying the fight is about over, that our side has lost. Hell, don't look that way around here."

Major Yaddow rubbed a hand across his face. "It's been a long fight, Leroy, I know, and you've been in it since the start. The hell of it is, we can't tell for sure how it's going. Sometimes we win and sometimes we lose. My boss is not feeling optimistic about things, I can tell. He never says, but I know. What we have to do is fight harder than ever and turn the tide in our favor once and for goddamn all time."

"Damn, I hope so. I'm still holding you to that nomination for U.S. Senate soon as we're a state. Damn, now that will be nice, Senator Smithson from the great slave state of Kansas."

"Yeah, Smithson, but that could be a long way off."

"You did promise me one of the nominations?"

"Hell, yes, but first we've got to smash down these damn northerners. That's first on our list, agreed?"

"Oh, damn right. The rest of my crew should be here about dark. When will your men be coming in?"

"About the same time, I'd guess."

"I better tell the cook to put on half a dozen chickens to roast and to cook up a big batch of potatoes and cabbage. That should fill them up."

The other five men from Smithson's persuasion squad straggled into the ranch just before dark. There was talk about the fire today in town and much guffawing and jokes made at the expense of the Deatherage family.

Smithson got his men all together and introduced them individually to Waddie Yaddow. Then they settled down in the big front room and listened to the man farthest up the line of the Blue Lodge, the southern forces in Kansas, that they had ever seen.

"You men are doing a fine job here. You're the troops in the trenches slugging it out with the enemy. And believe me, the northerners and the anti-slavery sympathizers are our enemies.

"What we do in the next year for certain will mean the difference in whether Kansas goes slave or free. Now, most of us don't want to use slaves. The economy of Kansas is such we can't plant cotton, and that's what slaves are best at harvesting. We're on the South's side for other good reasons. We have friends and relations in the South, we have strong cultural and business interests with Missouri, a fine slave state.

"We want to vote slave so we can stay in our proper area of influence, where we're comfortable, where we can make a good living, and where we don't let some damn bunch of northern slave-lovers telling us when to shit and brush our teeth."

There were some chuckles and a cheer or two.

"So what you men do here is tremendously important. I'm proud of you. I salute you. I am going to be forever in your debt when Kansas comes through as the slave state that it should be in the upcoming election.

"When is the election? Nobody is quite sure yet. It was put off once because we thought we could do better. There are some parts of Kansas not organized into counties yet, and we have to have that done before we can be a state. But the feeling is now that we should get the election going just as soon as we can, that it will be to our advantage not to put it off two or even three more years.

"That's one of the big reasons I'm here. Buckeye Springs has turned into a hotbed of northern activity. The leadership in Shawnee Mission has decided we have to make a stand here in this little town. What we want to do is burn it to the ground, every stick in the place."

There was a cheer from the eight men.

Yaddow grinned. "We want you men to help us. We have forty more men coming. We'll be heading out before long, but we'll give you all twenty-four hours' notice." He stopped and looked around. "Do you men have any questions?"

"Yeah, are you a real major?" one of the ranch-owners asked.

"Well, I'm as much of a major as Smithson here is a captain and you are a lieutenant. It's not an army rank, it's simply an organizational tool for a chain of command. Every army has one. Every big business has one. The important thing is that the system works, so we're not going to change it."

There were a few more questions, then the five men from the other ranches mounted up and rode out, still talking about the fun they would have burning Buckeye Springs to the ground.

About an hour later, Major Yaddow welcomed his other ten men, got them fed and bedded down, then went into the kitchen at the ranch house for some coffee.

"Smithson, I'm getting too old for this long riding," he said. "I don't mind a few miles, but all day is too much." He sipped the coffee.

Smithson grinned. "My friend, I have just the medicine to perk you up. Bring your coffee." They went up to the second floor and down three doors. Smithson didn't knock; he just pushed the door open and looked inside.

Fanny sat on her bed wearing nothing above the waist. She was drawing on a pad of paper.

Smithson pushed the door fully open and motioned

Major Yaddow inside. He took a step into the room and stopped when he saw the half-naked girl.

"Major Yaddow, I'd like you to meet Fanny, a bright, nicely made young lady who will be more than glad to help you relax after a long day's ride."

Fanny had not moved since the door opened. Now she smiled, made no effort to cover her breasts, and laughed softly.

"Major? A real major? Well, this calls for some expert and special service." She slid off the bed and walked toward him, her breasts jiggling and bouncing as she came.

The major's stare never left her chest.

"Well . . ." was all the major said before Fanny caught his hand and pushed it over one of her breasts. She nodded at Smithson, who chuckled softly and left the room, closing the door.

"Major, just relax. This is a little special magic-fingers massage I know that will make you feel just ever so much better. Come over here and lie down on the bed on your stomach. I have specially trained fingers, you'll soon see."

Yaddow went where she led him; he lay down and soon he felt her hands working on his back and shoulders, then his buttocks and his legs. By the time she turned him over he had an erection that was hard and throbbing.

Fanny had been talking since he came into the room, giving no chance for him to reply. Now she stopped talking and rolled him over on his back and at once pulled open his pants and pushed them down.

"My goodness, just look at that. A swelling. Major, we're just going to have to do something about that. That is, if it's all right?"

She bent close to Yaddow's face and he smiled and nodded. She kissed him hard and fast and then sat astride his torso and bent so one of her breasts flowed into his mouth. He sucked it in, chewing tenderly as her hands went down and played with his testicles in his scrotum.

He pushed her breast out of his mouth. "Girl, you better straddle that post down there you want any part of him. He's gonna blast off just any minute."

Fanny stripped off her silk panties and lifted over him and then sat down gently, guiding his lance straight upward into her waiting cavity. She squealed as she took him, then bent forward and stretched out her feet over him.

Gently she eased forward, then dropped back down on him, then up and forward again. A moment later the rhythm picked up and she rode him like a young stallion, her hips pumping and lifting, pumping and lifting, until the major cried out in delight that the big moment was at hand.

He grabbed her shoulders and held her tightly to him as he pumped his hips upward a dozen times, grunting and groaning and panting like a steam locomotive. When his passion was spent, he dropped his arms and she snuggled down on top of him.

"I like a good man pillow sometimes," she said.

Major Yaddow never even thought to ask her about her own climax. He drifted in and out of sleep and hardly knew when she lifted up and away from him. She covered him with a sheet, had a pull at a bottle of beer, and made sure that he was sleeping.

Then she eased onto bed beside him. Her hands, gently and without waking him, brought him back to a firm erection. She went over him and, positioning his erection precisely so, used it to twang her clitoris back and forth. The tenth time it triggered her and she billowed into a grinding climax.

Yaddow came awake. "I had the wildest dream," he said. Then he looked down at Fanny, still shattering herself in spasms of her continuing climax, and he grinned. "Damn, I'm still hard. Let's have another go." He pushed her on her back as her tremors still spasmed through her body and slammed into her hard and fast.

Damn but some men are dumb asses, she thought as she lay there accepting him. If she knew about men, this would be his last go. Then she could get some sleep. Vaguely she wondered what she had overheard from the dining room. They were going to burn down the whole town of Buckeye Springs?

She yawned and closed her eyes.

8

Canyon O'Grady watched J. A. Overbay closely. The man was lying. He was also the proprietor of the Overbay Dry Goods and Clothing Store on Main Street. It was the fifth stop that morning, and O'Grady was getting discouraged.

Overbay was a small man, thin, narrow-set eyes, sparse hair combed straight back with copper-rimmed half-eyeglasses perched on the end of his nose. He wore a dress shirt with the sleeves held up with elastic bands, and a necktie, but he had taken off his black suit coat jacket to help a customer with some clothing measurements.

There were no buyers in the small store, which was crowded between the general store and Lydia's Dressmaking, "cutting and fitting our specialty."

Overbay looked away from O'Grady, then he glanced back at the red-haired man. Canyon was not smiling.

"Mr. Overbay, I don't think you're being entirely truthful with me. What I asked is, are you now or have you ever paid someone here in town for protection for your store?"

Overbay's shoulder shook as he shivered, then his face showed his anger and his resignation.

"Yes! All right, I said it. That's what you wanted to hear. Why is everyone always threatening me? The man who came to see me was almost as big as you are. He told me I needed protection against drunks and raiders. Said he could guarantee that my store would not be vandalized or burned down. All it would cost me was two dollars a day.

"Sixty dollars a month! That's more profit than I make a lot of months. I told him I couldn't afford it. The man shrugged and walked out. That night my front window was smashed in. About fifty dollars' worth of hats and boots were stolen.

"The next day I found the man where he said he would be, and I paid him for protection, sixty dollars for a month in advance. Then I bought two new windows for the front of the store. I've got those two-foot-wide ones, set together, regular-sash-weight windows." Overbay walked over to the front of his store and looked out, then came back. "Since that day I haven't had a bit of trouble."

"And you think the person who broke in and stole the goods was the man who sold you the protection?" O'Grady asked.

"One time when he came to collect his monthly envelope of cash, he wore one of the hats that was stolen from my store. I know it was one of mine, but I didn't dare say anything."

"Mr. Overbay, this is important. I need you to tell me the name of the man you pay the protection money to."

Overbay shivered again and looked at the street. "He said he'd kill me if I ever told anyone, even my wife."

"Do you believe him?"

"Oh, yes!"

"How would he know it was you? There are forty merchants in town."

Overbay frowned as he thought about it. "Yes, yes, I see what you mean." He looked up at O'Grady. "If I told you, what would you do?"

"I'd have a talk with him, preferably with a gun in his ribs. I think the same man might have hung Mr. Rothmore, your neighbor here."

"Oh, God!"

"What I'm trying to do is track down a killer. He won't have any idea who has told me he's the one. I'm talking to every store-owner and merchant in town."

"That does help. Christ! What a problem. I hate that man. Hate what he's doing, but would I wind up dead if I told you?"

"I can't guarantee your safety, Mr. Overbay, but if I know who is the pickup man for the money, I'll get to his boss. Any idea who he's working for? Did he ever let slip a name?"

"Oh, no, never. Didn't even indicate he wasn't the whole operation. He always said 'I' and 'me'. Never 'we.'"

"Who is he, Mr. Overbay?"

The small man seemed to shrink even more. He sat down in a chair for people to use to try on shoes. He shook his head. "I should talk to Betty about this. She's my wife. I hate to make her a widow while she's so young." He stood and walked to the door and then came back.

"I've paid for seven months now, four hundred and twenty dollars. I'm slowly going broke. I can't afford that kind of a loss." He turned and now there was fire in his eyes. He marched up to O'Grady, who leaned against the counter.

"Damn, I'll do it. I can't more than lose the store. His name is Torris Canatale. He hangs out at the Hell Hole Saloon most of the time. He's an inch or two shorter than you, about six-foot-two, I'd say. Has a scar on his left cheek. Always wears a white hat with a high crown to make him look even bigger. He wears two six-guns so he has ten shots without reloading. Usually wears a fancy red vest and town clothes. String tie. One of his front teeth is missing. Oh, yeah. He has a handlebar mustache, otherwise clean-shaven and black-haired."

O'Grady chuckled. "I'd say you're right good at describing people."

"This one I am. I memorized every detail about

74

him, hoping I'd find some way to beat him without shooting him down from ambush. I never figured out a way.''

"Is he fast with his six-guns?" O'Grady asked.

"Not that I've heard. He never has to use them, just bluffs and threatens everyone because he's bigger than they are." Overbay grinned now. "Except for you. If you're planning a showdown with him, I'd sure like to see it.''

"You just might at that. Thanks. I'll leave by the back door just in case anyone is watching.''

O'Grady went to three more merchants that morning. Only one of them said that he had a contract with a private detective agency to safeguard his store. He wouldn't say who that was. Now O'Grady felt he was far enough away from the small dry-goods dealer, so he went across the street and into the Hell Hole Saloon.

It was eleven o'clock, and already the bar had a dozen patrons. Canyon ordered a beer at the stand-up bar and looked around casually. No one in the place could be Canatale. No man there was that big or had a white hat.

O'Grady finished his beer and stared at the empty mug a moment, then saw someone come in from the back door. The man was almost as tall as O'Grady's six-four, and he wore a high-crowned white hat that made him look a foot taller. He wore a gambler's red vest with a watch and chain across it. The man walked to a table where two other men sat, and dropped into a chair. When he turned, O'Grady saw a scar on the man's cheek: Torris Canatale.

Canyon nursed the last few swallows of his beer, then went over and watched a poker game for a few minutes. Torris and his friends sat at their table, working on bottles of beer and playing cards with no money on the table.

The big Irishman ordered another beer and pondered it as he tried to figure Torris. He worked for somebody. A man who looked the way he did—big and dumb—would not have the brains to figure out a protection scheme like this one. Who was behind it all?

If he followed Torris, the man should lead him to his boss. Eventually. But did O'Grady have that much time?

After another twenty minutes of nursing the beer, Canyon walked out of the saloon. On the other side of the street he saw some chairs outside a small butcher shop.

O'Grady settled in one of the chairs and tipped it back against the building so it rested on the rear two legs. Then he pulled his hat down so he could just see the street under the front brim.

The sun was pleasantly warm. Canyon thought of taking a nap, but at once knew he couldn't. Torris could leave at any time and he had to catch him.

The agent sat there for a half-hour, checked his pocket Waterbury, and closed his eyes for just a second. He burst them open with a grunt and then began counting people moving up and down the sidewalks to stay awake.

An hour later it was almost one o'clock, and O'Grady figured the big man and his friends would have to eat somewhere. Unless they were drinking their lunch. He had checked and the Hell Hole Saloon did not serve food.

By two o'clock, O'Grady still hadn't seen Torris come out of the saloon. He went over and checked quickly. Torris and his two men had left the saloon, probably by the back door, and walked up the alley.

O'Grady kept on walking up the street. He went past the small courthouse and the sheriff's office, but he didn't turn in. He'd been in situations where the local law had been more bother than good. In this town it was hard to know which side the sheriff was on. He got elected, so that must mean he was loyal to the South, since the pro-slavery candidates had won in the first election when all those volunteers crossed over from Missouri to vote illegally.

O'Grady kept on going and stopped at the town's small newspaper, *The Advocate*. He had seen the four-page paper that came out "once a week or whenever the news justifies." O'Grady knew that meant whenever they sold enough advertisements to make the paper possible.

The smell of ink and newsprint hit Canyon like a flash from the past as he stepped into the small newspaper office crushed between a lawyer's office and a real-estate and insurance firm.

The newsprint and ink smell brought up memories of O'Grady's fling with a newspaper in his early years. He saw a young man with a green visor reading proof on what looked like the front page.

"Help you?" the young man said without looking up.

"What is this, press day?"

"Indeed it is, and I'm an hour behind schedule."

O'Grady dropped a nickel in a tray and took a folded paper off the counter. "I'll just have one of last week's papers and let you work."

"Obliged," the editor/publisher said, again without looking away from the rows of print on the big proof of the front page.

O'Grady left the office and walked down Main until he found another chair, this one in the shade; he sat down and read part of every story in the paper. There was nothing even remotely touching on the North-South fight. He found a story of a wedding, one on the front page about the city council members who had decided that they would put up a standpipe to hold water for the city just as soon as they could afford it—and figure out how to pump the water into the big tank.

No mention of the arson fires in the area, no mention of the man killed a week before O'Grady came to town. It looked like the editor/publisher was trying to ignore the North-Sough controversy and stay alive and keep his newspaper publishing. But by not taking sides in the battle, he most likely would be subject to the wrath of both groups. It would be the "If you're not with us, you're against us" kind of logic.

Canyon watched as a man walked slowly down the middle of the street. He had a rifle over his shoulder and two revolvers, one on each hip in holsters.

A man on the boardwalk yelled at him. "Hey, Clyde, what the hell you doing?"

"Roving security guard," the man called Clyde said. "Sergeant has two of us inside town twenty-four hours a day. Part of our new town security system."

The man nodded. "Yeah, Clyde. Good for you. I'm keeping my Betsy rifle handy, just in case."

First, it was just night riders, O'Grady thought. Now they were setting up little armies. Where the hell would all this stop? From what he had heard in Washington last week, this North-South thing probably wouldn't stop in Kansas. The whole South seemed furious at the way things were going. Even some of the most conservative men in Washington were not ruling out that the South might carry out its threat to secede. That would mean war, the dirtiest of all the kinds of battle: civil war, with brother against brother, father against son. Somehow that must never happen.

O'Grady looked over at the Hell Hole Saloon and wished he could go back inside and check to see if Torris was there. It would be too obvious he was watching for someone if he did. The tall man didn't go back in the saloon from Main Street.

O'Grady began to feel hungry himself. He stopped at a small café and asked the owner to make him a roast-beef sandwich with a touch of horseradish sauce on it. That and a cup of coffee satisfied the redhead, and he went back to the boardwalk. Six men came marching down the middle of Main Street. They were two wide and three long, and Sergeant Luke Velman led them at a brisk pace.

O'Grady watched to see where they went. They stopped in front of the courthouse and Sergeant Velman talked to them for a moment, then all six hurried away to horses tied nearby. They paired up and two rode north, two east, and two to the south.

The sergeant came back toward where O'Grady stood by the general store. The ex-soldier paused as O'Grady looked up at him.

"Is that our security, Sergeant?"

"Indeed it is. A fine bunch of men. At least the pro-slavery clan won't catch us by surprise."

"Are there any rumors that they're going to attack?" O'Grady asked.

The sergeant looked up sharply. "Didn't say there was. But then I didn't say that there wasn't. Common sense the way things been going around here. Folks in this country think of Buckeye Springs as a northern free-state stronghold. The slavers are gonna come visit us sooner or later. I like to be prepared."

O'Grady nodded at the soldier. The sergeant lowered his head a fraction of an inch in reply and moved on down the street. Canyon felt a draft of cold air down the back of his neck. He had a unwelcome feeling that before this affair in Kansas was over, the whole nation would be plunged into a deadly, terrible civil war.

9

Canyon O'Grady spent the rest of the afternoon walking the streets, watching the door of the Hell Hole Saloon, and generally keeping his eyes open to find Torris Canatale. He saw nothing of him. He needed to know where Torris lived, but he couldn't risk asking anyone and tipping Canatale off to the possibility that someone suspected his part in the payoff racket.

Canyon checked in at the Hell Hole once more late in the afternoon, but Torris wasn't there. The place had no dance-hall girls and no rooms upstairs. It was a drinking-and-gambling saloon only. That cut down one possibility.

In the next hour, O'Grady went into the other saloons in town. There were seven of them. The biggest had girls upstairs, as did four of the others. Those would be spots to check later. By the time he got back to the general store it was nearly six o'clock and the closing hour. He walked in, and when Tabitha saw him, she smiled.

"Closing time," she said softly. There was only one man in the place trying to decide between eight-penny and ten-penny nails for his job. He at last chose the larger ones, bought a pound, and went out the front door.

Tabitha checked the store. No one else was there. She locked the front door and pulled down the blind. Then she walked quickly to the back and blew out the one lamp she had lit near the counter.

"My father used to say that this store is open whenever one of us was inside. If a customer could see you, you had to unlock and let him in even if you were stocking shelves or ordering more merchandise or trying to balance the cash box. Daddy was right. That customer is the most important element of the store. Without that customer, everything else I do, or can do, is worthless.''

Tabitha grinned and pushed the drape over the door to the storage room. She walked up to Canyon in the shadows and reached up for a kiss. It was warm and lasted a long time. When Tabitha at last pulled away, she sighed.

"Oh, my, that is nice. I hope you want to walk me home again. I feel downright dangerous tonight.''

O'Grady smiled. "Miss Tabitha, I'd be more than honored to walk you to your domicile.''

She snickered. "Good. Let's go. I want to show you how I've done some redecorating in the house. 'Course I get to buy everything at wholesale costs.''

They went into the alley where he settled his six-gun in its leather home. She took his left arm and they walked out the short way to the street and the two blocks to her house. It was just getting dark. The house was two stories, and in the faint light he couldn't tell what color the trim was to go with the white paint.

Inside, she closed the door and locked it. She reached for him and they kissed again, long and hard and then softer, more tender.

"Oh, Lordy, I'm going to die," she said, watching him. "Damn, I guess I should make us some dinner . . . before.''

He looked up at her and saw her grin. Then she lit a lamp and carried it to the kitchen, where she proceeded to cook him a steak dinner. "I bought this steak this afternoon at the meat market hoping you would stop by. Does that make me forward?''

"No. Your kisses take care of that nicely.''

"You're mean.''

"I only tease people I like. Rare on that steak, please. Don't fry it until it's dead.''

"Just the way you order it.''

They had supper a half-hour later. Mashed potatoes and beef gravy, carrots and peas, a mixed-fruit salad and rice pudding for desert.

After the meal O'Grady leaned back in his chair. "Best meal I've had in weeks. You're an excellent cook.''

"So marry me and settle down. I've got a store, lots of merchandise, good credit, and a great future.'' She grinned at him and then stuck out her tongue.

"You're also feisty, change your mind a lot, and you're still mad as hell about your father's murder. Let's get that cleared up first.''

She stood and led him into the living room. There was a long couch with soft pillows, a companion chair, and a fine view out the front window. She pulled the blinds and then settled down on the couch. He sat beside her.

"If you aren't going to marry me right away, we'll just have to pretend we're married.'' She grinned at him and leaned over and kissed him, her mouth open, waiting. She probed first, then withdrew, and his tongue followed.

She moaned softly and fumbled with the top of her dress. When the kiss ended, she caught one of his hands and moved it to her breasts. The dress was unbuttoned and she had lifted up her chemise so his hand could find her bare breast directly.

Tabitha sucked in a breath of surprise and desire as his fingers closed around her breast.

"Oh, Lord,'' she whispered, then kissed him again.

They lay back on the couch then, he partly on top of her, his hand still claiming her bare breast. He caressed it tenderly, working up to the nipple, which he felt and knew it was enlarging and filling with hot blood.

She pulled away from his mouth. "Mr. O'Grady, I

want you to know that I am not a loose woman. I have—have known a man or two in my life, but only at my choice and only when I was tremendously interested in the man.''

"I'm not asking any questions," he said. "Whatever you want us to do tonight will be fine with me, and I'll only respect you the more for it."

"Oh, good," she said, and kissed him again. Then she pushed him and they sat up. Her hands unbuttoned the shirt he wore and she laughed delightedly at the red hair on his chest.

"I was betting with myself that it would be red," she said, then she whispered, "Bet your crotch hair is red, too." She blushed and looked away as she said it.

O'Grady laughed. "Lass, you surely do have it right. Maybe later I can prove it to you."

She kissed him once more, then moved her hands to his belt and opened it.

"Not later, Canyon, love. Right now. I'm nothing but curious and hot and panting, and I want to see your good parts."

His hand massaged her breast, moved to the other one, and turned it to fire as well. Then he bent and kissed each one and he felt her jump from the excitement.

"Now don't rush me. I want to try something first." She opened his pants and pushed them as far down as she could. She looked at him and he lifted so she could push them down below his knees. She looked at the short underwear.

Without a word she pulled them down and grinned as his erection sprang up, hot and ready.

"Oh, yes," she squealed, "the good parts!"

She pulled the underwear off his knees and caught his erection with one hand and slowly stroked it downward, then up and down again.

She looked at him. "Is that interesting?"

"Anything a beautiful, sexy, half-undressed woman

wants to do to me is just fine with me. You have any more ideas?''

She stared at him. ''First I need to get out of some clothes.'' She flipped up the skirt of the dress and pulled it and the chemise off over her head and sat there, her big breasts still bouncing from the movement.

''Beautiful,'' Canyon breathed softly. ''The most beautiful part of any woman is her breasts. Just marvelous!''

''You may kiss them,'' she said. He did, then she pushed him away. ''Now for you, it's your turn first.'' She caught his penis in her right hand and pumped up and down on him a dozen times.

''You want me to . . . to come right here?'' he asked.

''Oh, yes! I've never seen it happen this way. Please?''

Without waiting his response, she bent and pulled his penis into her mouth, taking him halfway down, then coming off a little and bouncing up and down on him.

Before he could say anything, she lifted away from him and used her hand again.

''That was a little bonus,'' she said, her eyes bright. She pumped away at him now and he could feel the stirrings. O'Grady reached for her breasts and fondled one, caressing it, pinching her nipple, rubbing the orb gently, watching her begin to breathe faster.

''Yes, yes, I love it,'' she whispered. ''I love to see you get excited see your hips start to work.'' She pumped more and O'Grady let out a moan of pleasure, then the trapdoor opened and he humped upward with his hips as the raw fire of passion flooded his body and his hips jerked and pounded and the silvery creamy fluid spurted from his penis.

Tabitha stared in fascination as the fluid spouted from him. She counted out loud, and when she got to eight, he was finished. She wiped up the dampness with a hand towel and then bent and kissed his still-turgid tool.

"Tastes salty," she said, then snuggled down beside him on the narrow couch and kissed his cheek. "Thanks, I've never seen it happen that way before. Oh, I want you inside me, too, after you have a short rest.

"One boy I knew when I was sixteen said he could come six times in ten minutes and offered to prove it to me, but I didn't let him. He was a wild one. Were you wild when you were a young kid, Canyon O'Grady?"

"Not really. I always like to take my time with a beautiful lady, enjoy life to its fullest and a woman to her deepest."

She giggled. "You are bad, you know that? But then I guess I'm just as bad. No, not bad, I'm just normal female woman wanting some sex. I've heard some of the older women talk about having sex and babies and things. They are really bad."

"What do you mean?"

"Some of the younger married women say they like sex. They say their mothers told them they did it with their husbands on demand but never enjoyed it. I don't see how they could help but enjoy it. But the younger women, in their thirties, say the words like 'fuck,' and 'sex' and 'prick' and 'cunt' and all the other words. One woman said she insisted that she and her husband fuck every night after they got married until her husband finally gave up after a month. He could hardly drag around."

They both laughed.

"How many times is your record for one night, Tabitha?"

She grinned. "I was gonna lie and say four, but really it's only three."

"Want to break your record?"

She sat up and shook her breasts at him and pushed one toward his mouth. "Yeah, five or six, maybe seven.

I don't care if I'm sore for a week. You know I do get sore inside, but it doesn't last long and it's a wonderful place to be sore—I mean, it's more than worth it.''

"You have an alarm clock?"

"Sure, one I wind up and set to ring a bell." She grinned and punched him softly in the shoulder. "You mean we set it so if we go to sleep we can wake up and have another fuck?"

He laughed. "Absolutely. Get it now."

She took his hand. "Upstairs. My bedroom. We'll have more room on a big bed. A double bed, of course."

She led him upstairs as she carried the lighted lamp. Both were naked, and O'Grady figured if anyone were looking in the window they must have made an interesting parade through the living room and up the steps to the second floor.

Her bedroom was all pink and white, with chintz curtains and a fancy bedspread and big pillows with ruffles. The wallpaper was pink and the border a foot down from the ceiling was pink, but the ceiling paper was white.

Tabitha put the lighted lamp on the dresser and lit another one on a small stand by the bed and a third one on the far side of the bed. "I want to see every part of you all the time," she said, and jumped on the bed on her back and bounced. She spread her legs and held out her hands.

"Stand up," he said.

"What?"

"Stand up and I'll show you something new. Bet you've never made love standing up."

"Of course not. It can't be done." She grinned. "I tried once. Of course I was only sixteen and the boy was fifteen but taller than I was. We couldn't figure it out."

Canyon stood her up and pushed her against the wall. "Now, put your hands around my neck and lace

86

your fingers together and clasp your hands. Don't let go."

When she had done that, he bent slightly and picked her up by the thighs. "Clasp your legs around my waist and lock your ankles."

"This is going to be strange."

When she was in that position, he moved slightly away from her, lifted her hips forward, and positioned his lance at her magic entryway. Then he pushed in hard and fast.

Tabitha shrilled, a jolting yelp of surprise and some pain and a lot of wonder. Then she calmed and laughed softly. "Be damned, you're inside. So that's how it can be done standing up."

He reached down between them and found her clit and strummed it until she overflowed in one roaring climax after another. She was a screamer, and each new set of spasms that raced through her brought a wailing, screeching bellow of desire fulfilled and glorious and loud satisfaction. O'Grady had been with some women who merely whimpered once when they climaxed, and some like Tabitha, who let that whole end of the town know that she was in the midst of the wildest sex orgy of her life.

When she calmed, he wiped sweat from her forehead and laughed with her, then he pounded in and upward until there was no retreating. Tabitha tried to help but there was little she could do besides hang on.

When he billowed his second shot of the night, he turned and carried her to the bed in an awkward stiff-legged walk, then bent and rolled on the bed, but somehow the connection was broken and she yelped at her loss and rolled over him, kissing him soundly on the mouth.

She pushed away and lay on the bed watching him.

"Damnnn! Now that was a first." She cocked her head to one side and stared at him. "You have any more of them new fancy ways to fuck?"

"Maybe. You have the alarm clock?"

She bounced off the bed and brought it. Then she stood there, naked and small-waisted and good birthing-wide hips and bouncing breasts and a blond muff covering her crotch. "I've got some wine. I better bring up some. And some cheese and crackers, and some of them cookies I baked two days ago. Yeah!"

She turned and hurried to the door and he chuckled the way her round little bottom with the high buns bounced and wiggled as she vanished into the hall and the stairs. She came back at once, picked up a lighted lamp, and left again.

Four times that night the alarm went off. They woke up groggy and unsure, then saw each other and laughed and made love again and went to sleep and awoke again.

After the sixth time, Canyon pushed the button down on the alarm and they slept in to nearly seven o'clock the next morning.

Tabitha jumped out of bed and began to dress. "Oh, damn! I always open the store at seven-thirty."

"So you'll be a little late this morning. I'll get you some breakfast."

"No, no time. Thanks, I can just dress and make it." She stopped and looked at him. One breast was covered, the other stared out at him from under the edge of her chemise. "You have a hotel room? Why not stay here and save some money? Then, too, we could play married again—not six times a night, but you know, now and then."

"We'll talk about it. You get out of here and I'll leave a half-hour later by the back door as if I'm delivering something. You have your good name to consider here."

"Thanks. I still think fucking is fun." She giggled at her naughty word and her scandalous idea and hurried out of the bedroom tucking a pink blouse into her brown skirt.

10

The wagon with a man and a woman and two children in it came down the trail from the north. From the looks of the rig, the family had everything it owned on board. It was jammed and overloaded with furniture, mattresses, chairs, boxes, and a spare set of harness.

One of the Northern Guard Force men rode out to meet the rig. He had his rifle across his saddle. The second guard sat on his horse near the small tree they used as their lookout. His rifle was held to his shoulder aimed skyward, but ready.

" 'Morning," the guard said.

" 'Morning," the newcomer said. "You have trouble hereabouts? Why the rifles?"

"Just checking. Keeping the peace. Where you headed?"

The man frowned, then shrugged. "Moving from up country down to Buckeye Springs. Hear that's an up-and-coming community. I'm a cobbler. Always work for a good shoe man."

"We got one already."

"Usually room for two." The man hesitated. "You gents deputy sheriffs or something?"

"Nope. We're part of the Buckeye Springs Guard Force. Been some talk of a move by the southern sympathizers to sack our town. We don't aim to let that happen."

The newcomer hesitated. "It's come to that, has it? Armed guards, rifles, pitched battles." He sighed.

"Consarnit! Wished to blazes now that we'd stayed where we was in Iowa. Things settled down there good and proper. It's a state a'ready."

"What's your position on the slave question?" the guard asked.

"What? Slave? Ha. No man should ever own another man. That's about my position."

The guard smiled. "Well, glad to hear you say that. You're welcome in Buckeye Springs. Just follow the trail right on down. You're not more than two miles from town. About our cobbler: he's an old man, been thinking about selling out his little shop. Why'n't you go see him right off. His name is Goodenbaugh."

The newcomer smiled and nodded. "Well, now, that's really good news." He looked at his wife. "We appreciate it. Best get going before it gets any later. Much obliged."

The guard waved and the rig rolled forward.

That same morning, O'Grady went back on watch for Torris Canatale. The special federal agent was in and out of the Hell Hole Saloon as soon as it opened, but Torris wasn't there. He walked the town, then sat in front of the lumberyard. The place had little lumber, since it was bought up as fast as the man could freight it in from St. Louis.

O'Grady waited until nearly noon, then looked in the saloon again, bought a beer, and nursed it along.

Outside, he heard a commotion and he left to see what it was. Sergeant Velman had his troops in the street. They marched the length of the town with more than half of them keeping in step. When they came back, they did better.

The sergeant stopped them opposite the courthouse. The column of fours did a left-face, and when all men at last faced the right direction, Velman talked to them.

"Assembly time this morning took twenty-two minutes. Too damn long. We could be overrun by men with torches and the town could be burned half down. Work on it. Know where your men live and work or where they're going to be. This next week will be critical. We've had reports of men moving around, groups of men, armed men.

"I want to see the sergeants and the corporals here. The rest of you are dismissed."

The designated men gathered around the old sergeant. He spoke softer now, and O'Grady couldn't hear what he was saying. The men grinned and some chuckled, and then they grew more serious. A short time later they broke up and hurried off to work left undone when the call to arms came.

Twenty-two minutes wasn't bad, with lookouts two miles from town, O'Grady decided. He was impressed. Keeping a civilian force together was always a chore. The sergeant was doing a good job.

Another interested party was the gunsmith two doors down from the courthouse. He had kept above the hassle and gossip and backbiting of politics. But that was only a sham. He was a dedicated pro-slaver and a key lookout and undercover spy for Captain Smithson and his night rides.

He had to make a report. There was no way he could do it except making a ride south to the Smithson ranch. How could he do that with two of the guards down there watching the trails?

Fred Imhoff watched the men spreading out. He knew most of them . . . all of them. But this was a development that affected the work Captain Smithson was doing.

Hell, it would be helping the town as well. If Smithson knew there was a forty-man force here primed and loaded and ready to shoot, he'd be careful what he did. Certainly he wouldn't attack the town. So Fred figured he would be helping everyone in town as well by telling Smithson about the civilian army.

He even had a way to get through the screen of guards. He'd go hunting. Everyone knew he loved to hunt pheasants, and he was the best damn hunter in the county. He roamed far and wide to favorite spots.

This time he'd wind up near the Smithson farm. And he'd come back openly with his bag of birds. Yes, it would work.

He left shortly after ten o'clock that morning. He had a six-gun on his hip—he carried a weapon with him at all times, even when he went to church. In the boot of his saddle nestled his favorite double-barreled shotgun. He could bring down the most skitterish pheasant at thirty yards. Everyone knew him.

He found the two civil guards about a mile south of town near a small creek. They were fixing some food. He waved at them, then went over and talked.

"Stop anybody yet, boys?" Imhoff asked.

"Just you so far, Fred. Looks like you're hungry for pheasant."

"Damn straight I am. Then, too, I sell two or three to the Delmonico Restaurant. Helps pay for the shot. You boys want me to nail one for you?"

"Nope, we go off-duty at noon, so we'll get some good chow back at town."

"Tell your replacements that I came through so they expect me coming back. Heading down south another five miles to a spot I haven't hunted in six months. Should be ripe with just-matured birds."

"Imhoff, you own this whole damn county for hunting?" the other man asked.

"Just about. You find a man who wants to challenge me on a bird hunt and I'll lay a bet on myself."

Neither of the men took the challenge.

"Well, I better get moving or I won't get my count. I want six today. You men be careful of them night riders." He rode off with a grin. Fooled them completely. Damn, it was easy to make somebody think you were somebody or something that you weren't. Not about the hunting, he was the best shot in the county. But he fooled them about his real job down here.

He kept riding straight for the ranch. Two miles out he found an outrider from the ranch. They waved and Imhoff rode on in.

Smithson was just sitting down to noon food. "Where the hell's my pheasant?" he asked.

"Ain't had my gunner out of the boot yet. Got some news for you."

Smithson listened and then snorted. "Hell, they only got forty men. We got fifty and more coming. We aim to take that town apart—except your place, of course."

"How can you do that? My shop is right between two two-story buildings. I'll burn up quicker than a flash-powder charge."

"We'll try not to burn that side," Smithson said back-pedaling.

"Sure, you burn the business center and I'm dead. You give me some notice I can move my stuff out of the back door and get it to a safe place. All my guns and my machines."

"Yeah, but then everyone would know something was going to happen. Can't warn you, Fred."

Fred slapped the table with his hand. "I can't just sit by and let you burn me down, Smithson." He scowled at the captain, who had worked with him before. "Hell, guess I'll have to move to a little shack out at the edge of town where nobody has built another building right up against me. Some of the stores ain't so happy with me having all that gunpowder right downtown anyway."

"There you have it. Hire a couple of men and move out today and tomorrow."

"Why, Smithson? You coming into town the next day?"

"Could be. I don't give the orders. Major Yaddow is here from headquarters. I do what he tells me."

"But it will be soon?"

"Soon."

"Damn, I better get shooting so I can get back."

"Have some food first. Got some roast beef that's still good. You want a slab?"

Four hours later Fred Imhoff rode back into town with his six pheasant. He sold three to the restaurant

93

for fifty cents each, then dressed out the other three, gave two to his wife to put on to cook, and took the last one to a neighbor widow lady who could use the help. Twice she had offered to show him her bedroom. Each time she had a sexy expression, but Fred had one woman and she was enough.

He stopped in at two friends' houses and asked them to help him. Then he began moving his gunshop to a twelve-by-twenty-four building he owned nearly a quarter of a mile from his store. It stood on a corner lot with no other buildings within fifty feet of it.

He rented a wagon at the livery and had his second load put on board when his next-door neighbor merchant stopped by.

"At last we're getting this huge bomb out of the middle of town," he said.

"Joe, if you don't want to help me load all this stuff, get the hell out of here," Fred said, and grinned.

Joe helped with a metalworking machine Fred used to rebore rifles, and then slipped away.

They got most of the material moved by eight o'clock that night. Fred put the old sign up over the new store and left a note on the downtown door that he had moved. If Buckeye Springs burned to the ground, he didn't want to go down with it.

O'Grady had seen Torris Canatale twice that day. Once the man went into the Hell Hole Saloon, but Torris was gone by the time O'Grady could wander in. The second time Torris was heading into a bordello just down the side street from the corner on Main where the Kansas State Bank sat.

The man was more slippery than a fresh caught trout in bare hands.

Just at six o'clock O'Grady stopped by at the general store and talked Tabitha into going out for supper. They went to Delmonico's Restaurant and luxuriated in the deluxe dinner for sixty-five cents. It combined a slab of steak and two pieces of chicken, mashed potatoes and brown gravy, three kinds of vegetables, a green salad, a small loaf of bread they cut at the table, butter, honey, and jam, as well as coffee or tea and a huge piece of apple pie with fresh whipped cream on top.

Tabitha sat close beside him at the table and one of her hands wandered over to O'Grady's leg.

"Canyon, I really was swept away by last night," she said softly. "It was just wonderful. I'm hoping we can go back to my house for another try."

"First we have the town meeting," Canyon said. "You heard about the meeting Sergeant Velman called, didn't you?"

"Sure, but I didn't plan to go. We could get a bottle of wine and some cheese—"

"I need to go to the meeting. Maybe I can get a line on some of the local people who didn't like the marshal or your father."

"Oh, damn," Tabitha said softly, then she brightened. "But after the meeting . . . ?"

O'Grady grinned. "Sounds interesting. There must be a few ways we didn't try last night."

"I've got a couple of ideas," she said, grinning.

When the meal was over, they walked back to her house and inside. He reached for her and she came into his arms. The kiss was long and softly gentle. It was as if they had been there before and both were enjoying it again, now knowing the other person better, understanding their needs.

She snuggled against him and held him tightly with her arms around him.

"Just one problem," she said softly. "That one problem is that you walked into my life unannounced and unasked and I'm sure you'll walk out of my life the same way, quickly and without a lot of pain—at least on your part. When a woman gives herself to a man as I did last night, wholeheartedly, without any reservation, she has to pay a price; it costs her a lot whether she knows it or wants it to happen or not."

"Leaving is always hard," O'Grady said.

"But you do it. Sure, it's part of your job. You go wherever President Buchanan sends you, when he sends you. That leaves me, and I'm sure another girl or two around the country, high and dry and manless for months until we all can get over you and come back down to the ordinary, regular kind of man who is out there."

"Tabitha, you're a frank person."

She snuggled closer. "Frank, unmarried, and with no good prospects. I could have married this one guy six months ago. He took me out to dinner, brought me home, asked me if I could cook and if I owed any money on the store or the house, then he told me if I fucked good enough, he'd marry me. I hit him with a frying pan and he slammed out of the house so fast he forgot to take his hat."

"Now there was a frank person," Canyon said. He bent and kissed her. "I'll never ask you such an insensitive question. I already know." He kissed her again. "You want to go to the town meeting with me?"

"No. Too boring. I'll wait here for you, take a bath and get all beautiful for you."

She pushed him toward the door. "Now get out of here before I rip my clothes off and do something unladylike."

He pecked a kiss on her forehead, then left and headed for the Masonic Lodge Hall, where the meeting was to be held. It was the biggest building in town and could hold over two hundred, with most of them standing. By the time he got there, the place was half-full.

More came all the time. Most of them were men, but there were a few women with placards that read: "Women Vote Now," "Give Us a Say in Our Lives," "Women Voters Unite."

Five minutes before the called-for seven-thirty, Sergeant Velman went to a small stage and stood behind a podium. Slowly the crowd quieted down.

"Thank you, ladies and gents. This place looks bigger than the parade grounds at Fort Leavenworth. Most of you here tonight have come to help save our town. We don't want another Lawrence here. Some of you might be a little on one side or the other, but right now, the important thing is to save the town so we have something to vote about later.

"Without this town, we're all back in Ohio, or Pennsylvania or Nebraska or Missouri. First we defend this town. Raiders with torches are our biggest problem. This all-wooden-built town would burn up in an hour with the right wind and enough arsonists. We can't let that happen. Does anyone have any ideas what else we can do?"

A man up front lifted his hand. "How about using two lookouts in town at the highest points. The church belfry and the roof of the hotel?"

"Good idea, it'll be done. Anything else?"

"If this is gonna be a war, we need every man who can shoot a gun to be in our militia," an older man halfway back said. "Hell, I'm sixty, but I can see good and pull a trigger. I'll volunteer."

A small cheer went up.

"Another good idea. That is partly why I asked you men here tonight. We want to form three more forty-man companies of volunteers so we have a hundred and sixty men with guns ready to defend this town. What's this group's vote on the matter?"

A cheer went up.

"All opposed?" The women with the placards shouted no.

"The cheers have it," Velman said. "That's about it. Outside, you'll find three men who will serve as company sergeants. Now is the time to march out there and sign up with one of them. The first company we formed yesterday will be in formation with four rows of ten men to one side. Now is the time, let's move out men and find the squad you want to serve in."

O'Grady left and watched from across the street.

Most of the men at the meeting found a place in one of the three groups. Slowly the sergeants formed the men into squads of ten men, and within half an hour each sergeant had his forty men and had taken down names and addresses and working places.

Sergeant Velman stood on a fifty-gallon barrel on the porch of the gunsmith and shouted to the men. "Troops, atttentionnn!"

The men quieted and the sergeants got them all facing front.

"Congratulations. The men at the head of each row of four is a corporal and in charge of rounding up his three other men for drills and alerts. Before this formation breaks up, I want all of you to know where the other men in your squad work. The corporal is in charge of memorizing that information. We'll have an alert tomorrow evening at six P.M. I want you all here with your rifles and sidearms, ready to fight." He grinned. "We hope we won't have to fight, but we'll damn well be ready."

"Sergeants Boon and O'Connel, you'll post the six men to the forward lookouts and two to the in-town rooftops. That is all. This formation is dismissed."

O'Grady drifted away from the gathering. He wondered if he should stay the night at the hotel or at Tabitha's place. It wasn't much of a contest which one to pick. He went to his hotel room ready to get a clean shirt and a small bag of clothes and then move in with the sweet little lady for a while.

He started to put the key in his hotel-room door but noticed that it was partly open. Canyon drew his six-gun and cocked it, then rammed open the door.

Sitting in the chair by the window was Meg Ryson, the girl he had met on the train.

"Hi, O'Grady, quite a show they put on down there. I've been waiting for you to get back up here." She stood, and as she did, her blouse fell open, to reveal one pink-tipped breast.

Meg smiled. "It's good to see you again, O'Grady."

11

Canyon stopped and shook his head when he saw Meg Ryson standing by the window in his hotel room.

"What in the world are you doing here, Meg?"

She walked to him, her blouse slipped to the side until both her breasts showed. "I told you I might see you here when we were on the train, remember? I have some, er, business in this town." She heard someone in the hall and buttoned her blouse. "I told someone to meet me here for a few minutes, I hope you don't mind."

A firm hand knocked on the door and O'Grady lifted an eyebrow and went to see who it was. When he opened the door, he found Sergeant Velman standing there.

"I'm here to see Miss Ryson," the sergeant said.

O'Grady opened the door and waved him in. "Welcome to the Chicago Union Train Station, where everyone meets."

Sergeant Velman frowned at him, then saw Meg and walked into the room. The two nodded.

"Should he be here?" Velman asked.

Meg looked at O'Grady and then smiled. "Yes, I think it's all right. I know O'Grady from before, we have no secrets."

Sergeant Velman came to attention and nodded at Meg. "Very well. My report. I have 160 men here under arms and organized. We have a response time today of twenty-one minutes for assembly, but we'll cut that down. Do you have any news of the Southern Rovers?''

''Oh, yes, Sergeant. Too much news. They have expanded to forty men and were last seen heading this direction. Buckeye Springs now has developed a reputation around the state as a hotbed of northern sentiment nearly matching that of Lawrence. They'll come. We just have to be sure of the timing.''

''What about your own men?''

''Coming. Most of them will trickle in tomorrow. We don't want to make a public announcement. I have fifty riders, all well-armed. I've managed to get some of the new breech-loading rifles.''

''We'll need them. Will this be your headquarters?''

''Yes. I'll also use Room Twenty-two. I'll be watching your next assembly. When is it scheduled?''

''Tomorrow at six in the evening.''

''Good, gives me time to get organized. Any other problems?''

''No, ma'am. All else is under control. We've got security out three ways. Tomorrow I'll put out the fourth direction. Just wish to hell I knew where the Southern Rovers are.''

''We'll find them, Sergeant. I hope before they find us. Thanks for the report.''

Sergeant Velman saluted smartly, did an aboutface, and marched with military precision out the door.

O'Grady closed it gently. ''No wonder you said you might be coming to Buckeye Springs.''

''Business,'' Meg said, smiling.

''I'll be damned. You must be a general or something.''

''Something.'' She walked to the door, locked it, and pushed the straight-back chair under the knob.

Canyon shook his head as he grinned. ''I've never made love to a general before.''

Meg laughed, unbuttoned her blouse, and shrugged it off so she was naked on top.

''I'm not a general now, just a woman who wants

her man," Meg said. She caught O'Grady's sleeve and pulled him with her to the bed. They sat down, then fell backward. She lay there relaxed and unmoving.

"See how soft and compliant I'm being?" she asked. "I'm waiting for you to make all the advances."

"And it's killing you," Canyon said as he kissed her soft lips.

She yelped and reached for him and they both laughed. He lifted over her and kissed her flattened breasts and then her lips again.

"Slow and easy," he said. "I want to watch you undress."

She did, making it nearly a dance getting off her skirt and three petticoats and then the silk undergarment. She threw each aside until she at last was naked, all white and pink, with her dark-red hair with burnished gold highlights sweeping halfway down her back.

"Glad you didn't cut your hair," he said.

"Good to grab on to as you drag me around your cave," she said, and grinned. "At least we'll have more privacy and more room here than we had on that train coach seat."

"That was a first for me," O'Grady said. He shook his head. "I just can't get over the idea that you're one of the organizers of the northern antislavery forces."

"Why not? I was back East raising money just before I met you on the train. I did very well back there. We're winning here in Kansas, but the pro-slavers don't understand that yet. The ordinary people are tired of the looting and burning and killing. They want it finished quickly and the vote taken."

"How soon can the vote come?"

"Not for at least two years. Some of the counties aren't organized yet. That's why we have to hang on here." She shook her head and whirled her long hair around her face and shoulders. "I don't want to talk about that now."

"Then undress me," Canyon said.

The first time they made love so softly and gently that O'Grady figured that was the way it must be when you were married. Then they watched out the darkened window for a while, and when they came back together, Meg asked to be on top and it was a rampaging, grunting, passionate, and wild sexual encounter. They both lay on the bed still locked together and both panting and gasping for breath.

"Another one like that and I think I might die," Meg said, kissing his nose.

"You'll have company," Canyon said.

They rested and then at last sat up and kissed sweetly.

"We could always go to bed—and go to sleep," Meg said.

"Could always do that." He watched her. "You really have fifty more shooters riding in here tomorrow?"

"Yes. We want to put an end to the Southern Rovers. Those forty men have caused us more pain and suffering than any other band in the state. We want to shoot them up so bad they'll go limping back into Missouri."

"A real war?"

"If that's what it takes. We hope our advantage of more than four to one will convince them to scatter on their own."

"A lot of men are going to get killed."

"And maybe one woman. We all knew that when we signed on. It's part of the pledge of allegiance we take."

Canyon ran his finger around one breast, tweaked the nipple, and moved to the other orb. "You really think the North is going to win Kansas as a free state?"

"Absolutely. We're gaining votes with every day. We have people coming in from the North by the wagon train full. Give us another six months and we'll have the majority locked up here. The leaders of the southern groups are starting to worry. They want the election tomorrow; we say at least a year.''

''Damn. All I have to do is find a killer. You've got the hard job.''

''A killer? So you are some kind of a lawman.''

''Some kind. Have I ever shown you the Chinese Twist?''

''The what?'' she asked, laughing.

''The Chinese Twist position for making love. I think you'll like it.''

She did.

When morning came, Meg went to her room two doors down and dressed in a different outfit, a more mannish-type suit with shoulder pads and a straight jacket. They had breakfast in the hotel dining room, then Canyon went to find his best lead, Torris.

By ten o'clock he saw Torris coming out of the hardware store. O'Grady followed him. He went to the general store, then to the barber shop, and then back to a house two blocks down from Main Street. It was the Marshall Boardinghouse, according to a small sign on the door.

Canyon grinned. Damn, now he was getting somewhere. Torris was evidently having a meal there, and when he left, he contacted a small merchant. O'Grady saw them talking through the window, and when he went inside to ask if the tinsmith knew where he could find a good pocketknife, the two sounded as if they were in the middle of a good argument.

''I just don't make that kind of money yet,'' the merchant had said.

O'Grady looked around the store a minute, shook his head at the owner, and walked out. It had been a mistake to go in the store, but the idea that Torris was talking about money with the store-owner and the owner saying he didn't make that much profit, fell into line with the facts about Torris. He was the pickup man and now maybe the salesman as well.

O'Grady pretended to doze in a chair across the

street, his hat well down over his face. He spotted Canatale coming out of the tin-goods store and moving down three shops to a seamstress. He was in and out of there in a hurry, sucking on a spot on his arm.

The agent wondered if the stitching lady had jabbed him with a needle to urge him out the door.

The man made two more calls at stores before retreating to the Hell Hole Saloon.

O'Grady nodded gently to himself. He had the dog on a leash; all he had to do was watch him until he reported to his master, whoever that might be and whoever held the leash.

It was just before noon that O'Grady noticed strange men come riding into town. They came in ones and twos and threes. They tied up horses at various spots along Main Street. Some vanished into saloons, some walked the street looking in stores and shops.

About half of them went to restaurants and cafés for something to eat.

Promptly at one o'clock the men ambled down a side street and O'Grady wandered with them. Two blocks from Main they gathered and quickly formed into ranks and squads and a company. A sergeant stood in front of the men: five ranks of ten men each. A man rode up on horseback, spoke briefly with the sergeant, and waved three more horsemen forward.

The three rode up, took a salute from the other horseman. The one in the center was smaller than the others. Then O'Grady saw that it was Meg Ryson.

She rode to the center of the formation and spoke softly, and the ranks broke and the men crowded shoulder to shoulder in front and on the sides of her.

O'Grady moved forward as well. Her voice was firm, strong, as she spoke to the troops.

"Our intelligence riders have returned. They have tracked the Southern Rovers to a farm only a few miles from here. We'll form up first thing in the morning with our 210 men and attack that ranch just at daylight. This is the time we crush the Rovers forever and ruin them as a force in this struggle. I appreciate your dedication to our cause, your cause, and want you to know that this phase of it will be over, we prayerfully hope, within twenty-four hours.

"Now, we don't want to tax our friends here in town. Buy your own food at various eateries and let's camp out north of town a quarter of a mile along the creek. I'll see you at four A.M. right here and back in formation. We'll be taking a hundred and sixty of the town militia men with us."

A shout of joy went up from the men.

"Again, I thank you, the Northern Coalition for a Free Kansas thanks you. Now please move back into your ranks for dismissal."

The men moved at once.

Meg turned her horse, said something to the horseman who had first spoken with the sergeant. A moment later the sergeant dismissed the men.

All afternoon O'Grady watched for some sign of Torris, but he never spotted him. He must be sleeping or whoring or drinking. Maybe all three.

O'Grady watched the 160-man militia form up on Main Street at six that evening. They were all there and had reported to their sergeants by the appointed hour.

Sergeant Velman told them he had a surprise for them and then introduced them to Major Meg Ryson.

She gathered them around her, but this time, with so many, she had to speak much louder. "Gentlemen, I congratulate you on your formation of this militia. You men are the ones who will save your town and keep Kansas a free state. Tomorrow morning you'll have a chance to strike a blow for the freedom of all of the people of Kansas. Two hours before dawn we will meet here and ride to a ranch where there is a group of forty southern men determined to charge into Buckeye Springs and burn this town to the ground.

"We will strike first to prevent that, and to destroy a group known as the Southern Rovers. Yes, we will

105

leave twenty of the militia here to protect the town, and the rest will ride. Every man will come with forty rounds for his rifle and twenty for his revolver.

"Don't worry, I'll be riding with you, leading the charge. Now, get back to your homes, kiss your wives and sweethearts and tell them what we will do, and then get a good night's sleep. You'll need it tomorrow."

Dismissed, the men hurried home in a somber mood. The usual guards were stationed in the buildings and outside of town. Four men were sent two miles south of town in case any southern sympathizer tried to ride to the Smithson ranch to warn them.

The one man who might have tried to make that ride, Fred Imhoff, was still recovering from his trip to the Smithson ranch reporting the formation of the militia in Buckeye Springs.

He had worked well into the night getting his gunsmithing store moved out to the new location, and was so exahusted he hardly knew what had happened in the town. He heard about a town meeting but didn't go.

By the time he had the last load of his repair gear and merchandise out of the downtown store and put in the new store, he had nearly collapsed and struggled home.

Imhoff snored on the bed. His wife watched him, wondering if she should tell him about the town meeting. At last she figured it was better that he sleep. She had never been enthusiastic about his spying for the Southern Blue Lodge anyway. The way he sounded he'd be stove up half of the next day. She decided to let him sleep.

Meg had told O'Grady that she would meet him for supper at seven o'clock in the dining room. He had wondered why such a late hour but said nothing. Then he saw her at the militia muster. Now they ate and talked and he checked again to be sure that she was riding with the troops.

"I don't ride with them, O'Grady. I lead them on the charge. If I pick up a bullet or get killed, I'm perfectly ready to accept the consequences. What we're doing here is so damn important that I can't think of any other job that I could and would rather do."

Upstairs in her room, she kissed him and then pushed him away. "I have to set my alarm clock for three A.M. and get up that early, so I can't make love to you tonight. Tomorrow night we'll celebrate."

Canyon nodded, kissed her once more. "I'd like to ride with you, but, well, I can't. In my position I just can't take sides."

She signed. "Something like a judge. I accept that. Now get out of here and let me get some sleep. She took his hands and placed them on her breasts, then reached in and gave him a sexy openmouthed kiss before she pushed him out of her room as she pouted prettily.

O'Grady grinned. "A nice way to be booted out," he whispered. He walked down to his room. It was locked. Good. Now if there was no one already in his bed, he could get some sleep as well. He did.

12

O'Grady was in the street at four A.M. to watch the troops form up. Each man had a horse, each man had his rifle and pistol. Canyon walked along until he saw the troops all assembled and Major Meg Ryson rode out and took the report.

When she was sure that every man was ready to fight, she gave the command and led 190 men forward. Twenty of the militia remained stationed in town, an equal part at each of the four sides of Buckeye Springs to watch for southern raiders.

O'Grady wished he could ride along with Meg's army, to observe if nothing else. This was anarchy. He didn't see how the Territory of Kansas could ever become a state. Half the men would be killed off.

He went back to his hotel room and worried it for an hour, then got up from his bed and walked the town until the first café opened at six so he could have breakfast.

Meg led the men forward at a stiff walk. She knew it was nearly eight miles to the Smithson ranch and she wanted to capture any lookouts they had placed to the north and then sweep in unmolested to the farm. After scattering the men there, they would burn down the buildings and release any horses and cattle and chase any of the hostile southerners they could find.

That was the plan. As with any paramilitary operation, there is always some problem, some element that goes wrong.

It happened with the northern forces as they approached the first outpost set up by Smithson. They figured it would be three miles north, when in reality it was only a mile north of the ranch buildings. They sent out three men to subdue the outpost quietly, if possible.

The three-man team slipped up on the two men under the tree and captured one of them, but the second got off a harmless revolver round. He was blasted into hell by a pistol round, but there was a chance that the two shots had been heard at the ranch.

They were heard. One of the men in the haymow called out to the other guard, who alerted the foreman, and he told Smithson. Lights blossomed all over the ranch. Thirty men in the bunkhouse were routed out and put on alert.

Meg and her force came toward the ranch slower now. They saw the lights in every room of the house, lanterns hung outside, lights in the barn and bunkhouse.

They met no more guards by the time they were within three hundred yards of the place. Meg conferred with her military adviser, a man who once had been a colonel in the army and had fought the Indians.

Quietly an order went around. The troops were brought up into a "company" front and then each man was ordered to fire six rounds from his rifle into the buildings and the lights of the farmstead.

The resulting rifle fire raised a blue cloud of smoke, and when the rounds had been spent, the men were ordered to charge forward and sweep right through the barnyard, shooting at anyone on foot.

The line of inexperienced cavalrymen spurred forward. Some rode faster than others, some lagged behind, the line became a series of units at distorted angles, and soon some of the northern forces were between the ranch-yard buildings and friendly troops behind them.

The first dozen northern forces that swept through the yard found few lights still on and fewer targets.

Smithson had blown out all the lights when the rifle fire slammed into the house and other buildings. He had two men wounded already.

Major Yaddow was livid to think that his crack Southern Rovers had been caught off-guard this way. He stood in a shadow near the barn, and when the first mounted attackers swept past him, he fired five rounds at their backs, knocking one man off his horse and sending another one charging away screaming in pain.

Now one after another of the smaller segments of the northern forces swept through the barnyard.

Major Yaddow furiously tried to reload his percussion pistol. Just before he had the detonator caps pushed on the nipples, a rider spotted him and fired twice with his revolver as he raced past. The major took a .44 slug in the forehead and died as he vainly tried to lift his six-gun to fire at the attacker.

It took nearly ten minutes for the last of the northern troops to charge through the ranch yard. They assembled on the far side and Meg ordered half of them to dismount and find any cover they could and be ready for sunup, which should happen in four or five minutes.

She swung the mounted troops around to the side to give them a forty-degree angle of cross fire, and dismounted them for a continuous rifle-fire attack on the ranch buildings.

She sent two men running for the nearest barn; they came back a few minutes later, grinning. About that time smoke and flames burst out a back door and the entire barn seemed to explode with fire that roared like a tornado.

As soon as it was fully light, the men had found enough cover to hide behind, and the firing on the other barns and buildings began.

Two men from the ranch tried to get horses saddled in the corral, but they were shot down.

The men with Meg began taking some return fire from the intact barn and bunkhouse. Two men were hit.

"Concentrate your fire on those riflemen," Meg called. "Get the windows."

Twenty or thirty rounds jolted through the bunkhouse window and the two windows of the barn, and the return fire stopped.

"Cease fire," Meg bellowed. The call was picked up and the men on the other side of the barn heard it and soon all of the northern forces had stopped firing.

A white flag fluttered from a pitchfork out a small door, and a man came out slowly, holding the flag aloft. He had no weapon.

Meg sent Sergeant Petroff to talk to the man. The sergeant brought him back to the position where Meg crouched behind a small hump of dirt.

"Said he wouldn't talk with anybody but the general of this army," Sergeant Petroff told Meg.

She stood and stared at the man. "I'm in charge here. What do you have to say."

"A woman?" the man blustered. He got control of himself and shook his head. "I'm Elroy Smithson. These men took over my ranch and then you came shooting at us. There are six men dead in there, including a man calling himself Major Yaddow."

Meg looked up quickly. "Major Waddie Yaddow? Dead? Yes, I've heard of him. So, you're surrendering, Smithson?"

"Not me, I'm just a rancher. The rest of Yaddow's men want to give up. They say they'll ride out peacefully. Let them keep their weapons and their horses and they'll leave with no more gunfire."

Meg laughed. "Smithson, you must think I'm a fool. We've known for six months that you're the head of the local southern forces. We didn't know where Yaddow was. Now it's a neat package. We'll let you go back to your men with these instructions. They are to lay down all of their weapons in a neat stack in the middle of the ranch yard. Then they will form up into a column of four men wide. When you're in that position, we'll move in and take charge.''

"Young lady, we're not surrendering. All the men are asking for is a cease-fire. Enough have died today.''

"You didn't hear me, Smithson. We're in the commanding position. We can sit here all day, finish surrounding you, pick you off one by one. We have rations and water. We can pin you down until night and then charge in and finish you off.''

"You're the most bloodthirsty—''

"Smithson, we have a file on you. So far you've burned out six town houses, two businesses, and caused the death of six in the Andrews family. You call me bloodthirsty? You have a half-hour to meet my demands, otherwise we open fire again.''

Smithson stood there, the pitchfork tines resting on the ground.

"Get out of here, Smithson, your time is seeping away.''

Smithson turned and trotted back toward the barns.

Sergeant Petroff watched Meg. "You mean it about firing again?''

"If they don't form up in exactly twenty-eight minutes, we'll try to kill everyone of them.''

Only a few more shots were fired. One lone southern rider had put a halter on a horse and tried to slip it out of the corral riding barebacked.

Four rifles snarled and the rider and the horse both went down. The horse stumbled up, but the rider never moved.

Meg walked around the outskirts of her line of riflemen until she could see into the center of the ranch yard.

After fifteen minutes she saw a dozen men walking to a spot and laying down their weapons, then forming into a column of fours. She ordered her line of troops to move forward to within a hundred yards of the barn and wait.

When the half-hour was up, Meg counted over thirty men in the lines and saw a big stack of weapons in the yard.

"Mount up and move in," Meg called. "No firing unless fired upon. Let's go!" She mounted her animal and they rode forward at a walk. She made a motion with her hand and the troops on the other side of the buildings mounted and came in from that side.

Ten minutes later it was all settled down. They had captured thirty-four men. Seven had been killed and six had slipped away down a small ditch by crawling on their bellies.

Petroff was ordered to take identification from the seven dead men and give it to Meg, then bury them. As the graves were dug, Meg had men tie the rifles in bundles and load them on the spare horses. The revolvers and gun belts were stuffed in sacks from the Smithson barn and tied on another mount. They had forty-one horses as the spoils of war.

With that accomplished, the Smithson ranch buildings were burned to the ground. The forty-one horses from the Rovers were put on long lead lines and the northern forces led them back to town as the prisoners marched along cursing the heat and the dust and one another.

Sergeant Petroff rode up beside Meg and saluted. "Major, ma'am. There's blood on your trousers. Are you wounded?"

"It's just a scratch, Petroff, but thanks for your concern."

They marched a mile toward Buckeye Springs and stopped. Meg ordered ten of the prisoners out of the line of march. She stared at them from her perch on the big bay horse.

"I should order you ten shot as an example to the rest," she snarled at them. "But I won't. We're no maniacs in the North. We value human life, we don't make slaves of other humans. So you ten are free. You will turn to the east and walk, run, or crawl until you get to the Missouri border. It's less than fifty miles here. Go, now!''

The ten men looked at one another. One shrugged. One stepped out to the east, then another one did. Soon all ten were running away from the formation straight east.

Each mile up the road she released ten more until all of the Southern Rovers were dashing for their lives across the fields and prairie toward Missouri.

Meg settled into the saddle. ''Let's move out a little faster, Sergeant Petroff. We should be back in Buckeye Springs in time for a good midday meal.''

O'Grady picked up Canatale about ten that morning coming from his boardinghouse. He went down the street and directly into the Hell Hole Saloon, which opened at ten. O'Grady decided now was the time; he pushed through the saloon doors, got a beer, and looked around. Torris and another man were already at a game of cards at a back table.

O'Grady moved that way, clinking five twenty-dollar gold pieces in one hand. He watched the game a minute, clicking the coins.

Torris looked up.

''Want some fresh money in the game?'' O'Grady asked.

''Hell, no,'' Torris said.

The other man, older and a little on the heavy side, held out his hand. ''Wait a minute. The gentleman comes with coin of the realm good and pure. Why not let him sit in a few hands?''

Torris shrugged.

They were playing with cash on the table. O'Grady fished in his pocket for all the coins he had besides the double eagles, and piled them in front of a chair and sat down.

The older man shuffled the cards. ''Dollar limit to start?'' he asked. O'Grady nodded. ''Dollar ante,'' the dealer said. "Five-card draw, jacks or better and no progressive."

O'Grady couldn't open. Nobody could. They threw in the cards, sweetened the pot, and O'Grady dealt. He saw that the cards were marked but only slightly. He dealt straight because he couldn't read the marks.

The older man opened for five dollars. O'Grady laughed and folded. So did Torris.

"You guys are no fun," the older man said. "The idea is to bet."

"I saw you in the tinsmith store yesterday," Torris said, staring at O'Grady.

"Oh? I didn't notice you. I was looking for a new pocketknife, but figured he didn't have any. Found a good one at the general store."

A half-hour later, Canyon had lost ten dollars. He had finished his beer. He snorted in disgust and pushed back from the table. "Ten dollars is my limit these days," he said. "Maybe tomorrow."

"Fresh money is always welcome," the older man said as O'Grady walked away. He had learned what he wanted to about Torris Canatale: the man was not overly bright, he did not know how to play poker very well, and he would not scare or bluff easily.

Canyon went to the general store and picked out three cheap hats in different colors, a dull-green shirt and a bright-blue one. If he was going to trail Torris until he found out who the man worked for, he needed some different clothes that the mark hadn't seen before.

Tabitha stalked up, arms folded, formal and distant and then pouty as another customer left the store. She stood in front of him and frowned. "I thought you were coming to see me last night, and then I missed you all day yesterday."

"Busy, sweet Tabitha. I do have to do some work so I can keep my job, right? I'm working on finding the killer and I think I'm getting closer."

"How about tonight?"

"I'll make it if I can, but I'm following this Torris guy to find out who he works for. That's why I need the strange clothes."

She warmed. "Oh, I see. Good idea. I don't have to charge you for these"

"Of course you do. The government is paying. Now, let me wait a few minutes in front of your store watching for him. I'll be there tonight if I can make it."

O'Grady paid for the clothes, then waited in the front of the general store near the window watching the saloon. After five minutes, he changed his mind and went into the alley behind the Hell Hole and watched the back door where the drunks came out to use the one outhouse.

A half-hour after O'Grady settled down in back of two big packing crates, he saw Torris come out. He looked both ways, then hurried up the alley past O'Grady's hiding spot and into the back door of the second building from the street. After a reasonable time to assure himself that the target wasn't coming back out, O'Grady checked the store from the front.

It wasn't a retail store, it was a lawyer's office. J. Mulligan, Attorney at Law. The U.S. government agent crossed the street and walked into the meat market so he could watch the lawyer's office. Why in hell would a man like Torris go into a lawyer's office?

13

It was an hour after O'Grady spotted Canatale going into the lawyer's office that he saw him again. Torris came out of the Hell Hole Saloon and headed back toward his rooming house. He took a detour and stopped in at the door on the courthouse marked, SHERIFF'S OFFICE.

O'Grady leaned against the First Kansas Bank and lifted his brows. Now, there was an interesting development. Before he had time to think what to do, a thundering army of horsemen galloped down Main Street. At the head of them rode Major Meg Ryson. The group didn't look too badly shot up. He saw two horses with bodies draped over them and tied on. Several more men showed white bandages around wounds.

Meg brought the men to a halt and Sergeant Petroff ordered them to do a left turn so they faced Meg.

"Well done, men. I'm returning the control of the Buckeye Springs militia to Sergeant Velman. He'll carry on with his security here. I'm proud of you citizen-soldiers—proud that each one of you is doing your patriotic duty.

"There are still a few of the Southern Rovers out there and they might try a counterattack to satisfy their own anger, so we must be ready. My men will stay in town for about a week to be sure things are settled down. Again, thanks, men, you were glorious out there today."

Sergeant Petroff took command and dismissed the

troops. They screeched in delight and half of them mobbed the nearest saloons.

Meg stepped down from her mount and gave her to a trooper, who led the animal away.

Canyon fell into step beside the woman as she headed down the street toward the hotel. "Ma'am, would it be all right if I ordered up a hot bath for you?"

Meg looked over and grinned. Her face was dusty and smudged with dirt and residue from the smoke of the gunpowder. Her hair straggled down in half a dozen streamers from where she had pinned it up under her cowboy hat. She limped slightly and looked ready to stumble.

He put out his arm and she took it, flashing him a grateful smile.

"About that bath. Oh, yes, yes. But I'm not sure I can stay awake long enough to keep from drowning. I'm going to need some help."

"I'll call the sergeant. I'm sure he has one of his men who would be—"

She hit him with her small fist in the shoulder. "O'Grady, I want *you* to help me, you silly!"

"Shocking, Miss Ryson, absolutely shocking!" O'Grady grinned. "And wildly exciting. With you so exhausted, I might be able to take some wild liberties with you."

She grinned up at him. "O'Grady, I might be sleeping at the time, so you won't get credit for any points scored."

"Oh, damn. To change the subject, what do you know about the sheriff in this county?"

"Harry Loughran. He was a gunfighter once in Texas, had a small reputation there, nearly got jailed in Arizona for murder, and showed up here with the land rush in fifty-four and ran for sheriff. His opponent fell and broke his arm one dark night and he suddenly decided to move back to Illinois. Loughran was elected. As far as we know, he hasn't taken either side in the slavery issue.''

''An honest lawman?''

''Possible, but with his background, doubtful.''

In the hotel, Canyon went to the desk and ordered six buckets of hot water to the second-floor bathroom and four big soft towels. A silver dollar traded hands and the clerk called to one of the young men who worked there.

The bathwater arrived at the bathroom just after Meg and O'Grady did. He poured it in, four buckets of hot and two of cold. He locked the door and helped her out of her dusty shirt and the chemise she had tucked into her pants. Her breasts bounced and winked at him, and he couldn't help but reach in and kiss them both.

When her pants came down, he saw the blood and then the wound on her thigh.

''You didn't tell me you'd been shot,'' O'Grady said sternly. ''We better get you to the doctor.''

''Not until I'm presentable. Besides, it isn't that bad. The bullet went right on through.''

''But it hurts, right?''

''Like nothing I've ever felt before. That's why I got my wounded men to the doctor first.''

Canyon used one of the towels and wiped away the blood and looked at the wound. It had taken about two inches of flesh and poked a hole straight through. Dried blood caked on one side, the other side oozed a little fresh blood.

''You'll live. Right now it makes you sexier than hell.'' He stepped back and looked at her naked form. ''Delightful,'' he said. ''Sure and there's nothing I'd rather do than unwrap a pretty package like you are, lass.''

''Thank you.'' Meg posed prettily for him for a moment naked, then stepped into the tub. ''Now wash my back before I die.''

It wasn't supposed to be a sexy bath and they both

sensed it. She washed her breasts and legs and he poured water over her after she had washed her hair. He tenderly cleaned the blood off her leg so he didn't open the wound. Then he dried her leg and put on a bandage compress of one of her clean handkerchiefs and used some strips torn from his red handkerchief to bind it firmly in place.

"You better have the doctor check that today or tomorrow. We don't want it to get infected," Canyon said.

"He's busy enough today with my wounded. Anyway, I'm too tired."

He helped finish washing her legs and found the robe she had brought from her room.

"See, you helped give me a bath and we acted just like old married folks," she said. "I don't feel like lusting after you at all."

"That's because you're the one naked and I'm not," O'Grady said with a small laugh. "I could give you an equal chance to see me naked, too."

She shook her head. He helped her out of the tub and dried her off, then she slipped into a robe and they went back to her room. She dropped on the bed and he pulled a light cover over her.

"Now, you sleep for about six hours. That's an order," O'Grady said. "I need to go meet the sheriff and see what kind of a man he is."

"You be careful," she said as her eyes fluttered shut.

"Always." He bent and kissed her forehead and he saw she was sleeping already.

A few minutes later, Canyon stepped into the sheriff's office and saw the usual: a small room with a counter across it and two desks behind it. No separate room for the sheriff.

The man who sat at the larger desk was tall and thin, with a full beard cut close. He looked up at O'Grady with cold green eyes and nodded.

" 'Afternoon."

" 'Afternoon. You the sheriff?"

" 'Pear to be."

"Just the man I want to talk to. I'm looking for a job. You got room for any more deputies here?"

Sheriff Loughran laughed. "Got only one now, and the city fathers want me to cut back on his pay. Don't reckon I can put on another one, lest you want to work for free."

"Hadn't planned on that. I done some law work down in Texas and a bit in Arizona. I can handle a gun and a horse, and most men, unless they're too big or professional bare-knuckle pugilists."

The sheriff looked at him. "Reckon you could at that. Shame, in a way. I hired a man just last month. Sorry. No way I can help you. One of the saloons sometimes is looking for a bouncer."

O'Grady shook his head. "Not my style of work. Well . . ." He stood up. "Thanks for your time. I'll probably be moving on down the trail somewhere. Maybe back to Texas. This damn Kansas is crazy, all these good people fighting one another. I never heard tell of such goings-on."

"If you plan on staying in Kansas, better get used to it. This feuding is set to last for a long, long time down the trail."

O'Grady waved and walked out of the office. It had no jail, no deputy in evidence, and evidently only one on the payroll. He probably worked at night. So why was Torris coming to call on the lawman? Then, why was Torris going to see a lawyer?

Canyon left the sheriff's office and walked up the street and, without thinking about it, ambled into the general store. Tabitha watched him come down the middle aisle between the hoes and rakes and racks of horse collars. Her arms were folded defiantly across her chest and her chin tilted up just a little.

When he came close enough, he saw that her eyes were now hard as jade and snapping at him.

"I saw you walking that female general to the hotel," Tabitha said, ice dripping from the words.

"She's something of a local hero here in town, don't you know? She and the Buckeye Springs army took on the Southern Rovers and ran them into the prairie."

"She seemed most friendly and familiar with you."

"I was surprised to see her here. We met on the train coming out from the East. We sat near each other in the coach."

"Oh!" Tabitha's anger seemed to fade. "In the coach. I just thought that . . ." She frowned a minute, then threw up her hands. "Oh, damn. I can't be mad at you. When I saw her holding on to your arm . . . Well, I just thought—"

"She'd been up for almost twenty-four hours and had just led her troops in a battle, and she was wounded in the leg with a rifle round. She needed some help to get to the hotel."

"Okay, all right. Forget it. I'm sorry I was snippish." She motioned him to the back. "We do have something else to talk about. I had a visitor this afternoon, not more than an hour ago."

"Let me guess. Was it Torris Canatale?"

She scowled and twisted up her face. "How in the world did you know?"

"I've been following him. I'm sure now that he's the one contacting the merchants, but I don't know who his boss is."

"We talked. He said he knew that I was all alone and that so many bad things could happen. He guaranteed me protection for only two dollars a day."

"What did you tell him?"

"At first I was so angry that I nearly shot him. I had the double-barreled shotgun on the counter shelf, where he couldn't see it. I just nearly picked it up and fired."

"Glad you didn't."

"I told him that his guard service was too expensive, that I might be able to afford one dollar a day, but I'd have to talk to the man he worked for first. I told him I didn't deal with underlings. I said I'd be willing to listen to reasons why I should take the protection if the head man of his group met me tonight here at the store at six-thirty.

"Torris said the head man never contacted the customers. I said, Fine, then I won't be a customer. He left saying he'd talk to the boss and tell me later whether the head man would be here."

"Good work, we should hire you on as a crime investigator. I'll want to be here when whoever it is comes. I'll be in the shadows somewhere so he won't see me."

"I was hoping that you could be here. I'll have my shotgun and my forty-four, but sometimes it's hard to scare a man who is carrying a gun himself. You noticed that Torris has been packing a revolver these last two or three days."

"I noticed. That's a change. Must mean something."

"Maybe they're getting scared."

"Of what? It could be he's scared of the southern raiders."

"Could be."

"I'm overdue at the stables. Cormac needs a good run. I've been neglecting him. I'll be back well before six-thirty. I'll come in the back door."

She reached out and caught his hand. "O'Grady, thanks." She looked up. "Then, too, I'd really love to have you at the house tonight."

"I'll do my best, little lady. Do my best."

Cormac began stomping in his stall when he smelled O'Grady. The big palomino would hardly stand still to be saddled. He took the apple O'Grady bought from a grocer on his way past, and chomped it up almost before he knew he had it. Then the stallion nuzzled O'Grady for some sugar.

"When we get back, big lad. You get your treat after you show me you can still run."

They went out of town to the north at a gentle trot; then, when past the last house, O'Grady nudged the big bronze horse with the pure white tail and mane, and he dug in his hind quarters and slammed down the dirt road.

O'Grady galloped him at full speed for a quarter of a mile, then eased off to a trot and a walk as they turned back toward town. Canyon rode all the way around the settlement and came back to the north again, then to the livery. They had ridden about two miles.

O'Grady gave the stable boy a dollar to be sure to take good care of Cormac, then paid another week's feed and stable bill and fed the big pale bronze animal a quart of oats. When the oats were gone, Cormac nuzzled O'Grady again, and this time it brought out the lumps of sugar he had picked up at the grocery store. The big horse ate them and looked for more.

"Next time, old friend," Canyon said. He scratched the mount behind the ears and headed back for Main Street. His Waterbury showed him that it was just five-thirty.

The Buckeye Springs militia was changing the guard, sending out scouts at the four points of the compass and shifting the lookouts in the tall buildings. There was bound to be some reaction from the Southern Rovers, but first they would have to find horses and rifles. That could take a day or two.

O'Grady went into one of the smaller saloons and watched a poker game. It was not good poker and he moved to another table where the stakes were higher and the men were not just learning the game. He watched and tried to figure out who was bluffing and who had the cards. Twice he guessed on the big bluffer and twice he was wrong.

That's why he wasn't a better poker player than he was. He had to learn how to read a good player. The poor ones gave away their hands almost when they picked up their cards. It was the man who knew how to keep a poker face and to bid the same way whether he had the cards or not, that made a poker player a winning poker player.

O'Grady checked his watch. Twenty minutes after six. He left the saloon and wandered down Main to the first cross street and walked quickly up the alley to the general store's back door. It was unlocked. He slipped inside and threw the locking bar, then moved quietly toward the half-light coming through the door to the front of the store.

Tabitha walked past the door and spoke softly. "I heard you come in, O'Grady. That is you, isn't it?"

"O'Grady reporting for duty."

"Good. It's almost six-thirty. I've left the front door open. Oh, oh. Here comes someone now. I can't see who it is. I'll be by the counter with the weapons within easy reach."

"I'm here to back you up." O'Grady watched carefully through the open door to the back room as someone opened the front door and walked into the general store.

14

Canyon O'Grady watched the man walk from the dimness of the front door of the store back into the light of the counter area, where two lighted lamps burned. With a surge of disappointment, O'Grady saw that the man was Torris Canatale.

Tabitha recognized him before O'Grady could and she folded her arms over her chest. "What are you doing back here, Canatale? I told you to send your boss."

"I am the boss, I run this business."

"Not a chance, Canatale. You're not smart enough to put something like this together. Now, get out of here and tell your boss it's no sale. And if anything happens to my store, if even one small window gets broken, I'll find you and blow a hole through you."

Canatale relaxed and leaned against the counter not quite in arm's reach of her.

"No such thing, woman. I'm here to tell you that you owe me sixty dollars for the first month. You pay me now and we won't have no trouble at all."

Faster than O'Grady thought possible, Tabitha pulled the six-gun from under the counter and cocked the hammer. "You want to say anything more or do I just shoot right now?" she asked with scorn.

Torris Canatale eased back from the counter, his hand moving down his side.

"Don't move that hand any farther, Torris," Tabitha spat. He never stopped the movement. Tabitha pulled the trigger and the five-shot revolver barked out a deadly warning. She had lifted the muzzle so it aimed at his right shoulder, and the round hit him exactly there, staggering him back two feet.

"Bitch," he roared. "Little lady, you'll be lucky to be alive by morning. Nobody—I say nobody—shoots Torris Canatale and gets away with it."

"Big talk. Ease that six-gun out of leather and drop it on the floor, right now." Tabitha cocked the hammer on the next round and Torris stared at the weapon. His left hand had grabbed his shoulder to try to stop the bleeding.

"Drop it or take another round. Your choice," Tabitha said.

"Goddamn—"

"Being an outlaw and a thief is harder now than it used to be, Torris. Drop the iron or I shoot you again."

Slowly his left hand crossed over and lifted the weapon out of leather by the butt and he bent and laid it on the floor.

"Now, turn around and walk out of here, slow and easy. I'll be six feet behind you with another round a finger twitch away. Move!"

Canatale shuffled toward the door. "You'll regret this, Rothmore."

"Why? Did you help hang my father?"

He looked over his shoulder in surprise, then hurried out the front door.

O'Grady watched her lock the door, then come back. She picked up the gunman's weapon and looked at it. Canyon met her at the counter. "I'd suggest we both stay right here tonight," he said. "We're damn sure going to have a visit from Torris or whoever he's working for. Nice shooting."

"My daddy taught me to shoot when I was ten. I got pretty good. You don't forget something like that." She frowned. "You think they'll try to burn us out?"

"No. Too many of their clients would get ruined and that would cut off some of their income. They'll try to smash the front windows and turn the inside of the store into a trash heap.''

''Oh, dear! How do we stop them?''

''Firepower. You still have that sawed-off shotgun?''

''Yes.''

''Good! I'll use it. Get me a box of double-ought buck shells. What is it, a ten-gauge?''

She brought back the shells. The little weapon already had two double-ought buck rounds in it. He hefted the shotgun and grinned. ''Now we wait. Your friend will go see the doctor, then hire himself about three men and come back, probably after midnight. Be surprised if anyone came before then, but they will come.''

''And they'll smash the front windows?''

''To get in. I figure we'll let them smash the windows to be sure they're serious, then I'll unlimber the little shotgun and prove to them how serious we are.''

O'Grady watched her. ''You had any supper yet?'' She shook her head. ''You hang on here. I'll go over to the café and bring us back some supper and a bottle of whiskey, and then we'll wait. At least we don't have to miss supper.''

Two hours later they had eaten the steak dinners he carried in on the café china. He also brought a pot full of hot coffee and the whiskey.

Canyon moved near the front behind the rack of horse collars. He could see past them and they would give him some protection. He checked his Waterbury with a scratched match. It was just after eleven o'clock. All the lights were out in the store.

Less than an hour later, he saw a shadow come across the front door. Someone tested the door handle, then tried a key in the lock. A solid two-by-four and sturdy strap metal barred the front door. Outside Canyon heard someone swearing.

A moment later a rock or a brick crashed through one of the front windows. The window was two feet wide and three feet high, and there were three of them side by side on each side of the front door.

O'Grady heard voice outside. The first hesitant foot came to the window and kicked out the rest of the glass and a man stepped in. Canyon waited. Right behind him came another man. Now! O'Grady aimed low and fired. The fifteen .32-caliber slugs from one barrel blasted forward and swept the legs out from under both the men.

They screamed in terror. One crawled out past the jagged window glass to the boardwalk.

"You, shot-up burglar. Don't move or you're dead. You hear me?"

The man lying against the far wall with his legs pulverized stared into the darkness. He had been wailing in pain. Now he nodded. "Yeah, I hear. Don't shoot again."

"I will unless you tell me who hired you?"

"Easy. Torris Canatale."

A pistol fired from outside and the man jolted as the slug hit him.

O'Grady leapt to the broken window and looked out. He saw a man running down the street thirty yards away. The agent fired the second round from the other barrel at the figure, but he vanished in the darkness.

There was little need to check the burglar. When O'Grady did, he found him dead. The .44 slug had hit him in the side of the head.

Two men from the saloon across the street hurried over. "What happened? Wasn't that a shotgun I heard?"

"Go get the sheriff," O'Grady said. "We've got some business for him here. Then, too, you better also bring the undertaker. The doctor is going to have a man with some shot-up legs as well."

The two men hurried off.

"Is it over?" asked Tabitha.

"For now. If that was Torris, he got away. He sent his lackeys in first."

"They broke my window."

"Just one. If you have some glass, I can replace that in the morning. You got off lucky this time."

"Who is behind all of this? Is it somebody here in town? Maybe one of the other merchants?"

"You know the town, I can't help you there." O'Grady brought up two lamps and lit them and sat them in the window next to the dead man. Then he unbarred the front door and stepped outside. Most of the window glass has showered into the store. Down the street he saw two men walking toward him. He reloaded the shotgun and held it easy.

"Deputy Pendleton here, you with the scatter gun. Just keep that thing aimed down."

"Figure to do that. You checked the doctor yet? Should be a man there with slugs in his legs. I want to talk to him."

"Later. You got a body here?" Pendleton asked.

O'Grady told him what had happened, showed him the evidence. "I was talking with him when the man who hired him stood outside in the dark and killed him with a pistol shot to the head. Easy to see where the slug went in. My six-gun hasn't been fired, in case you're interested. Know this man?"

"Yep, he's Utah Bob. Always kept telling us how he was going back to Utah. Caged drinks at the saloons. Never had a job I know of. You say there were two others?"

O'Grady told him the story again. "Now you take care of things here, I want to see if the doctor has been busy tonight."

"Hold on," the deputy said. "How do I know you didn't kill this man?"

"Because I was here and saw the whole thing, Deputy," Tabitha said, coming up out of the shadows. "You know me. This is my store. A man threatened me tonight, so we waited until he came back to burn us down. We stopped him, and then, when his man

130

was still alive, the one who threatened me shot his hired hand to shut him up.''

The deputy nodded. ''Could be. I want both of you to come to the sheriff's office in the morning and file a statement.''

''Tomorrow,'' O'Grady said, and hurried off toward the doctor's office. It was a Main Street office; the doctor lived in back and the lights were on.

O'Grady tried the front door and it was unlocked. Inside, he heard two men talking in the next room. He moved silently and looked in the door. A man sat on a low table with the doctor in a chair binding up both the patient's legs. He had his pants cut up each leg.

O'Grady drew his six-gun and walked into the room. ''So, we meet again. How did you get your legs shot up that way, stranger?''

''Now see here . . .'' the doctor began, then stopped when he saw the weapon. The other man was under thirty, had a mustache and short cut, dark hair. He looked away. O'Grady had never seen him before.

''I got caught in a gunfight in a saloon,'' the man on the table said.

''Not likely. The sheriff just told me it had been a quiet night, no shooting except one tonight.''

''So . . .''

''So, who hired you to smash that window on the general store and go in and trash up the place?''

''I wasn't there.''

''Those shotgun wounds testify that you were there. Looks like you're done, Doc. I'll see that this gent gets safely to his boardinghouse.''

''No! I won't go outside with you.''

''I won't treat you nearly as bad as the guy who hired you will when he catches you. You know he killed your buddy inside the store, don't you?''

The bandaged man's head snapped up. ''No!''

''Yep. He's deader than a buzzard's breakfast. Shot him in the side of the head with his forty-four. I bet when he sees you, he'll do the same with you. Torris is that way."

Again the man's head came up sharply.

O'Grady lowered the six-gun. "You want to tell me what he offered you two? You got to be damn careful to stay away from Torris tonight or you'll be in hell with your buddy and waste all the doctor's work on your legs."

"Christ, I can't even walk."

"Yeah, tough. Make it easy for Torris to blow your head off. He hire you?"

"Yeah."

"He tell you why?"

"No, just to break the window and go in and tear up the place, wreck the inside but not to set it on fire."

"He going to help?" Canyon asked.

"Said he'd stand guard outside."

'Considerate of him. Thanks. Oh, you got any money left?"

"Little. Why?"

"You owe the store-owner five dollars to replace that window."

"Yeah. I got two dollars."

"Close enough." O'Grady took the two dollars and stuffed them in his pocket. "Don't forget to pay the doctor." He walked out the door and then jogged down the street to the general store. The undertaker was just hauling away the body. O'Grady went inside and found a piece of tin roofing that would cover the front window. He nailed it in place on the outside and went back inside.

Tabitha watched him. "Will Torris come back here tonight?" she asked.

"I doubt it. Especially since he heard that dead man tell me who hired him. He's one angry delivery boy right now. Just wish I knew who he was reporting to. It would save a lot of work."

Canyon paced the aisle. "This is coming to an explosion point, Tabitha. I'm going to have to track down Torris tonight. I know where he lives. Will you be all right here for a while?''

''Yes. Give me the shotgun. I know how to use it.''

''Back door is safe enough. If Torris comes back, it would be through the front windows, but I don't think he will. He's probably got a slug still in his shoulder and is hurting like fire.''

O'Grady found the shotgun where he had put it before he left the store, and gave it to her. ''I've got a couple of places to check. Just keep watch until daylight. I should be back long before then. I'll call out before I knock on the front door.''

Tabitha reached up and kissed his cheek. ''I don't know how to thank you,'' she said.

O'Grady laughed softly. ''I bet you remember one way you can thank me. Now hold fast. I'll be back as soon as I can.''

Canyon went out the front door and waited for her to place the bar in the holders. Then he checked his six-gun and ran down Main Street toward the boardinghouse where Torris lived. Chances were it would be dark, with everyone sleeping. He'd have to wake up someone and find out if Canatale was there.

When O'Grady came around the corner near the boardinghouse, he saw that it wasn't dark. There were lights on in the downstairs and in one of the upstairs rooms. The agent grinned. Maybe this was going to be easier than he had thought. He headed for the front door, changed his mind, and slipped up to the living-room window and looked inside the boardinghouse.

15

The thin curtains didn't hide much inside the board-inghouse living room. Torris Canatale sat astride a turned-around wooden chair with his shirt off. A woman in her forties dabbed at his bloody shoulder and jawed at him to hold still. Torris yelped every time she touched his wound.

O'Grady grinned and slid around the house without a sound. Almost no one locked their doors these days. He found the back door open and eased it inward. There was a small room for overshoes and raincoats and sheepskin coats, and then another door. It must lead into the kitchen.

Canyon tried it without a sound. He prayed that the hinges didn't squeak. They were silent as he opened the panel. He stepped into the kitchen with his six-gun up and ready. He had five loads in the cylinders and caps in place. As he moved forward to the edge of the kitchen, he could hear the two talking in the living room.

"Hell, it was a lucky shot. I didn't think she would shoot. Little bit of a thing. She'll pay. Tonight, she'll pay. No matter what he says, I just might burn her out anyway."

"That will get you in big trouble, you said so."

"Don't care. Nobody, nobody shoots Torris Cana-tale and gets away with it. I'm gonna kill that little bitch."

"Better get permission first. He'll be damned mad at you. Things are just settling down around here."

"Who cares? Ouch! Dammit, be careful."

Canyon looked around the doorjamb at the living room. Now! The big Irishman ran three steps into the room with his six-gun trained on the pair. "Easy now. Lady, you put your hands on top of your head and move over about three feet. I'd hate to get you splattered with any more blood."

"Bastard!"

"Stand up, Torris. We're going for a walk. Lady, if you leave this house while we're outside, I'll come back and burn it to the ground, you hear me?"

"Yes." Her face was tight and hard. She'd seen danger before.

"Torris, on your feet, out this way. You won't need a shirt, it's warm out tonight. A good Kansas fall night. Move!"

Canatale lifted off the chair. His shoulder had only a small compress over a wound and one or two wraps of bandage. It would have to do.

"The back door, we're going for a walk."

"If I don't go?"

"I shoot you here, splatter what you call your brains all over the lady's new wallpaper. You don't want that, do you, Torris?"

They went outside slowly, O'Grady two steps behind, Torris with his hands laced together on top of his head. Once outside, O'Grady waved him to the south. They would be out of town in a quarter of a mile.

"So, you killed one of your helpers tonight, but the other one got to the doctor. Too bad, Torris. You had a nice little racket going here. Who set it up for you?"

Canatale walked ahead without a word. O'Grady moved up behind him and slammed the butt of his .44 into Torris' right kidney; he slumped to his knees, bellowed in rage and pain, and vomited.

O'Grady waited six feet away, the weapon still in his hand, the trigger cocked again. "I'll ask nice once more, Torris, then we get messy. Who are you working for on this merchant-protection racket?"

"I ain't—"

135

"Careful what you say, Torris. You aren't in any position to argue or bargain with me. Give me the name and your game is over. I'll lock you in a barn somewhere until I can take you to Kansas City on federal charges."

"Can't tell you. He'd—"

"But he isn't here, Torris. I am. I'll do twice as bad as you can imagine that he might do. I'll be in no rush. He'll be furious and do it quick. You want fast or slow? Now, or maybe tomorrow? Don't think too long. I don't have much time."

"Hell, it's a legal guard service. Nothing illegal about it at all. I checked with a lawyer."

"Not when you use intimidation, threats, and violence, and not when you hang a merchant at his own front door. All of that is against the law, Torris. Who is the boss?"

Torris sat in the dirt looking up at O'Grady.

"Get up, we're going out a ways where nobody will bother us. We'll see how good you are at taking pain. I knew this Indian . . . now, there was a man who knew how to get the most pain out of a person in the shortest period of time. The Comanche are really artists when it comes to torture. He taught me his whole bag of tricks."

Torris got up and walked. He looked at both sides of the small street, but by now there was only one house per block, and soon there were none. The street gave out and they walked into the unbroken prairie.

"Damn, I wish the sun was up. Then I could spread-eagle you on the ground, tie you down, and cut your eyelids off. Takes only about an hour to fry your eyeballs and make you permanently blind. But no sun. I'll think of something else."

Torris tried to run. He charged to the side and went ten feet before O'Grady shot him in one leg. He went down and rolled in the dirt.

"Nice try, Torris. Now, who is your boss? Who's making a thousand dollars a week and giving you fifteen dollars? Is it the banker?" Torris shook his head.

136

"I'm not going through every name in town," Canyon said.

"I'll never tell you. Go ahead and kill me."

"Not a chance." O'Grady tapped the barrel of his revolver on the wounded shoulder. Torris bellowed in agony. He shook his head and whirled around, then bleated at the pain in his left leg.

"How much can you bleed and stay alive, Torris? Any idea? I heard about a pint. I'm not sure. Want to find out?"

Torris roared in fury and clawed at O'Grady; he jumped up and even on his wounded leg took three steps toward the agent before he stumbled and fell into the dirt and the dry fall grass of the plains.

"Stupid, Torris. You're just plain stupid. Here you are getting pushed around, shot, pounded on, eating dirt out here in the prairie, and your boss is sitting with some woman back in town lifting a glass of sipping whiskey and humping his favorite lady again. Why should he have all the fun?"

"Yeah. Okay. If I tell you, I get to go back to the house?"

"Maybe. You got some money stashed there? You fucking the landlady?"

"Yeah. But you won't put me in jail here?"

"Don't know if that would be good. Hear there hasn't been a trial here in two years."

"Just so you don't put me in the county jail."

O'Grady heard raw terror in the man's voice. What did he have against the jail? "I didn't know they had any jail cells here." O'Grady nodded. "Why don't you want to be in the jail in Buckeye Springs? Don't you like Sheriff Loughran?"

Torris' head snapped up quickly. "He don't like me. He might beat me up if I was in his jail. He just don't like me."

"Okay, Torris, I won't put you in his jail. Now, who is this bastard who's milking the businessmen dry and who hanged Rothmore?"

"It's him." Torris shivered and turned toward O'Grady. "Oh, God, but I feel sick. I'm gonna throw up again. Oh, damn! Help me."

O'Grady frowned, but bent lower so he could see the man better. In that fraction of a second, Torris exploded upward, pushing off with his good leg, swinging a four-inch knife with his left hand.

O'Grady lunged backward but couldn't escape the blade. It sliced a shallow groove across his upper chest, missed his throat, but cut deeply into his left arm.

By the time O'Grady had jumped back and kicked at the knife, Torris had slashed again. The big .44 came swinging up and O'Grady fired once by instinct, a responsive reaction. The slug rammed into Torris just below his rib cage and churned up his intestines before lodging somewhere in his lower back.

Torris fell to one side and the knife dropped from his hand. "Bastard, you gut-shot me," he said.

O'Grady pulled out his handkerchief and wrapped it around his left upper arm, where the blade had bit into his flesh. It should stop the bleeding.

"I didn't think you looked like a knife man. I was wrong this time, but at least not dead wrong."

"You gut-shot me!"

"Which means you're a dead man. It might take a half-hour, it might take two hours, and it's going to hurt like you've never hurt before."

"I've seen a man die that way."

"So buy your way out. You tell me all you know about your boss and I'll leave you one round in a forty-five derringer."

"You're crazy. Why would I want to do that. Hell, bastard, you shot me! I won't be doing you any fucking favors."

"I was thinking about a favor to yourself. So, we sit here and wait. Unless you want to walk back into town."

"Then I could die in bed."

"Give it a try."

Torris started to lift his legs to sit up when he bellowed a scream of pain, agony, and rage all melded together.

"Oh, I forgot to tell you. The pain from a gut shot is a lot worse if you move around. Walking is impossible."

Sweat started to seep down Torris' face. He glared at O'Grady. "Just who the hell are you?"

"I work with the United States government. I'm a special agent assigned by the president."

"No shit. Why you here?"

"To find out who killed U.S. Marshal J. B. Tippit."

"Damn, told him that was a mistake."

"The mistake was having three other bullets in him, especially those that entered his back."

"You know that, too?"

"Your undertaker may not be the best-liked man in town, but he was upset by the way the marshal was murdered. Your round from the front didn't kill him. It was any of the other three that did it."

"I told the guy we shouldn't do that marshal so fast. Why did he come to town?"

"Letter from your friend Tabitha. She knew somebody killed her father. She wanted justice done."

Torris trembled, biting his lip to stop the pain. He shivered and then groaned as wave after wave of pain cascaded through his body and slammed into his brain. He gasped for a minute, then looked over at O'Grady, who sat six feet away on the grassy plains of Kansas.

"It gets worse than this?" Torris asked.

"One hell of a lot worse."

"Okay, the deal. The derringer, and I tell you all of it, agreed?"

"Right. This is the little gun. I'll take out one round. Now talk."

"The boss. The one making all the money. Damn, I should have figured it out and taken more. He's the county sheriff, Harry Loughran. Came up with the idea about a year ago and worked it slow. He's got about twenty-five signed up so far. We've had to break into ten of the firms and smash them up a little.''

''What about Rothmore?''

''He was tough, paid awhile, then quit and said he was going to talk everyone else into quitting. Loughran said we had to make an example of him. We caught him coming out the back of his store that night, knocked him out, then hung him from the front about three in the morning. Took him a long time to strangle.''

''Sheriff Loughran ordered you to help hang Stanley Rothmore, right?''

''Right. Oh, damn!'' Torris curled into a ball and screamed as the pains drilled into him again and again and again. When he could, he sat up. ''Can we speed this up?''

''Then the U.S. marshal came to town and checked in with the local law, and the next day he was dead.''

''Right. The sheriff said we had to work fast before he found out a damn thing. I got three drunks and drifters to hide in the back room and we practiced, and then, when I picked a fight with the guy Tippit, I backed him right up to the curtain and they all fired at the same time.''

''Again, on orders of Sheriff Loughran?''

Yes, dammit, yes, What more do you need?''

''Where are the other three men? I want them, too.''

''I paid them what Loughran gave me for them, twenty dollars a man, and chased them out of town the next day. Don't know where the hell they are by now.''

''I guess that has to take care of it.'' O'Grady stood, moved back another three feet, and lay the derringer on a grassy spot. ''There it is. You can move that far. I'll be well out of range. You've got just one shot, don't waste it.''

O'Grady lifted up and walked quickly back toward town. He turned and saw Torris pick up the gun. He put the short barrel in his mouth and pulled the trigger. The muffled explosion of the round filled the night for a moment. Torris slammed backward.

O'Grady continued on into town. In this case it wouldn't do him any good to build up a tight legal case. There was no law and order, not in Ashland County. Now, how did he deal with a legally elected county sheriff who was a murderer and an extortionist?

Canyon walked slowly back to town, avoided the boardinghouse, and stopped in front of the general store.

"Tabitha?" he called. He called twice at the front door and was about to leave when he heard the bar come away and the panel open a crack.

"O'Grady?"

"Yes."

She pushed open the door and he slipped inside and put the bar back across the holders.

"Tell me about it," she said. She took his hand, sensing that he had solved part of the puzzle. She led him back to the counter, where she had spread out six horse blankets. A lamp burned softly. She sat on the blankets and tugged at his hand to pull him down beside him.

"It's almost over. I know it all now."

Tabitha shivered and pushed over beside him and snuggled against him. She closed her eyes. "Tell me, I want to know everything."

He went through his fight with Torris and the walk into the prairie and how only one of them walked back.

"The pain must be terrible," she said.

"The men who killed your father were Sheriff Loughran and Torris. He admitted it. Now all I have to do is arrest the sheriff and lock him in his own jail."

"But we don't have any judges. There hasn't been a trial in this county in almost two years. It won't do any good to arrest him."

"As soon as I can, I'll take him to Kansas City,

141

over the line in Missouri. There I'll charge him on a federal warrant. He'll get hung in Missouri.''

"I hope." She snuggled closer. "O'Grady . . .''

He bent and kissed her lips. "Right here?''

"Why not? You getting bashful?''

"Not so you would notice, lass, not so you would notice.''

She turned and he saw that she already had her blouse unbuttoned. She found his hand and slid it inside the cloth and purred as he caressed her breasts.

"I'm so glad that you came and that you've found out who killed Daddy. It shouldn't have happened.''

"Sheriff Loughran never should have pressured him so hard about the protection racket.''

"Don't talk so much." She kissed him again, then they leaned back and lay down on the thick stack of blankets.

She pulled and wriggled out of her clothes. "Tonight I want to be all bare and naked and you touching me all over so I feel wonderful," Tabitha said.

She undressed him and then rolled on top of Canyon. The heat of her body warmed him as she played with him, explored, giggled; then at last, puffing and breathing hard, she lifted up and came down on his lance until their pelvic bones ground together.

"Oh, yes, home at last," Tabitha said. She provided the motion and soon she squealed and panted and roared into six surging climaxes. She panted and gasped for breath and settled down on top of him in total rapture. Then she lifted up. "Oh, did you make it?''

Canyon laughed. "In there somewhere between those twenty orgasms you had. Relax, have a nap.''

O'Grady held her and thought through the assignment. It hadn't turned out the way he figured it might. The Kansas burning was a real surprise to him. He knew there was trouble out here, but not like this. No wonder the sheriff didn't take sides. He was making

142

more money than all of the paid gunmen on both sides. He couldn't afford to get involved.

O'Grady drifted off to sleep, awoke briefly when Tabitha slid off him and cuddled against him on the thick blankets.

For just a minute he wondered what Meg Ryson was doing. She was recuperating from her shot-up leg, for one thing. He hadn't seen her in a day, a day and a half. She would be furious. He'd find her tomorrow and make it up to her. If he wasn't too tired . . .

He put his hands behind his head and thought about the case again. The sheriff? Had to be. He was in the perfect position to do the dirty work and not take any argument. He could close down a store, run the owner out of town, sell his place for taxes. He had the whip to rule the roost.

But now the chickens were out of the coop. First thing tomorrow morning he'd go pay a call on the sheriff.

O'Grady must have slept after that. He came awake stiff and found Tabitha partly on top of him with one of her hands cupping his genitals.

Something had roused him. Then he heard it again, a horse pounding down the street. He sat upright when he heard three shots in quick succession outside.

"Everybody to his post," a voice outside shouted. "The Southern Rovers are riding this way. They killed Willy Burnose out at the southern outpost. Everyone up, they'll be here in about twenty minutes."

The revolver fired three more times, and by then O'Grady had his pants on. He wouldn't be taking sides if he was helping to defend the town.

Tabitha sat up in a fuzzy fog.

"Get dressed," he told her. "The Southern Rovers are attacking the town. They'll be here soon."

16

Canyon repeated the words, knowing that Tabitha, who still sat on the blankets with her bare breasts bouncing from her movement, had not quite come awake yet.

"The Southern Rovers are attacking the town. We have maybe fifteen minutes. Get dressed and tell me how to get on the roof."

She jumped up and grabbed at her clothes. "Roof, yes, ladder up the back. Rifles are in the front rack and shells. Take one of the new ones."

"Get dressed and lock both doors and don't let anyone inside."

O'Grady grabbed one of the breech-loading rifles and a box of shells to fit it and hurried out the back door. He spotted the ladder and climbed it quickly, then ran to the front of the gently sloping roof to the false front, which rose nearly two stories.

He kicked a board loose near the roof level so he could see the street and down it toward the south.

In the street below the companies of the militia began to form up. Within ten minutes, nearly half of them were there. Sergeant Luke Velman sent half the men to the first houses at the southern edge of town and told them to set up in a line of skirmishers across the south trail, fifty yards on each side.

"Find something to protect you, a wagon, a house, a box, or some dirt, and get settled in to start shooting." He sent fifty men out there with two of his new sergeants. "Start shooting when they get within a hundred yards," he ordered them.

He found ten more men and told them to get horses. They would ride out a quarter of a mile beyond the skirmishers and wait in two groups on each side of the trail, out of sight if possible, and ambush the Southern Rovers as they came toward their positions.

By that time more men surged into the formations, and Meg Ryson was there with her Sergeant Petroff and his men. They put them on roofs at the southern end of town and organized a twenty-man cavalry unit to be used for pursuit if the Rovers turned and ran.

Then a calm settled down over the small town of Buckeye Springs.

Ten minutes later a rider came back from the south shouting the news. "We can see a dust trail. They must be coming. No contact yet." He turned at the far end of town after repeating his message in a town-crier manner and rode back to the south. A few minutes later he rode back and O'Grady could hear shooting at the far edge of town.

Canyon wished that he had set up farther to the south. It could be all over before anyone got this far. He shrugged. It really wasn't his fight. It would be best if the superior force could route the Rovers with a spanking and not a lot of casualties.

O'Grady moved to the south side of the store and climbed up on the false front so he could see over the next store. He had a perfect view a half-mile down the south road.

For a moment he saw a flash of riders, then heard shots and saw more riders heading south. A pall of blue smoke showed until it was blown away by the always-present Kansas east wind.

There seemed to be nothing happening for several minutes, then the line of men at the far end of the village began to fire. Half a dozen horses on the road quickly were turned and raced away. A horseman galloped into town to the end of Main Street, and a moment later the twenty cavalry riders surged around the corner of one of the stores and raced down the south road.

They swept past the line of skirmishers and on down to the south, evidently after the Rovers.

Ten minutes later, from far off, O'Grady heard some shots, but not a lot. He decided the battle of Buckeye Springs was over, so he took his rifle and box of rounds and climbed down the ladder to the back door of the general store. He banged on the door.

"Yes?" Tabitha asked through the wood.

"O'Grady here, lass. I think our war is over."

She opened the door and let him in. They went through the store and out on Main Street. Dozens of people ventured out to look south and to exchange what news they knew.

"It's all over," a man shouted as he rode down Main.

"Must be our new town crier," Tabitha said.

On the way back he stopped and elaborated to a group of about twenty-five people.

"Our first line cavalry surprised them and forced them back down the road," the man said. "Then I guess the Rovers slipped around our front cavalry and first thing we knew the Rovers were at the outskirts of the town. When they got within a hundred yards, our boys fired.

"By that time there were about fifteen of the Rovers. Our Fifty men blasted them. Knocked four of them off horses and killed them dead. Put down two more horses and ran them Southern Rovers down the south road in a rush.

"Then Sergeant Petroff brought his cavalry troop and kept up the pressure, chasing them halfway back to Tennessee."

"Any casualties on our side?" someone asked.

"Near as we can tell, we had four wounded and one of the first cavalry unit was shot dead. Outside of that, it's a big victory for us."

O'Grady looked down at Tabitha. "I wonder if the gent who got killed feels that way," he said softly.

She shushed him with a little grin.

By then the first of the troops were coming back to town. They didn't march, they just walked in an elongated mass. The first fifty started to fall into ranks, then shrugged and most of them headed for the saloons.

The horsemen rode back in with one body over his saddle. He was taken to the undertaker.

Six wounded men lined up outside the doctor's office.

Meg rode in a half-hour later with the twenty-man cavalry unit. They looked a little grim. She dismissed them and Sergeant Petroff talked with her for a few minutes, then she gave him her horse and came up to where O'Grady and Tabitha stood.

"Is it really over?" Tabitha asked.

Meg looked at her and then up at O'Grady. She gave a sigh. "We hope so. We have lookouts in the field down the south road and around town. If they try to come again, we'll know it. But, no, I don't think they'll try again. They're hurting too much. They lost more men; they're down to about ten men. We only lost one."

"I'm glad it's over," Tabitha said.

Meg glanced at her, then up at the redhead standing beside her. "Is your name O'Grady?"

"Guilty," he said.

"Would you mind if I had a private word with you? One of my men says he recognized you. It'll only take a moment."

"I need to get back to the store," Tabitha said. "I forgot to lock it when I left. Excuse me." She walked away but looked over her shoulder with a frown as she hurried back to the general store.

Meg looked up, the weariness seeming to drop away. "That was just an excuse to get rid of her. Can you come back to the hotel with me? There are some things I want to show you."

"I thought I'd seen all of your things," O'Grady said.

She laughed. "True, but these are documents, orders, authorizations."

"Sounds important. I would, but first I need to set up a meeting between a store-owner and the sheriff. He's one of the rats in this town and I've just about got enough evidence to hang him. But I need a little bit more. "How about a date for tonight, about eight o'clock in your room."

"Sounds good. Gives me time to take a bath and then a nap. Don't be late. I'll have our midnight snack all ready."

O'Grady waved and walked into the general store. He did want to have Tabitha try to get Sheriff Loughran to admit that he was selling the protection in town. That might be quite a job, but it was worth a try. It would be solid evidence he could take to Kansas City with the prisoner for his trial.

Ten minutes later he had told Tabitha his plan. She finished waiting on a customer, and when he had left, she nodded. "All right, I'll try it. I'm not good at this playacting, but I think I can do what you suggest. I'll send a note to the sheriff and see if he takes the bait. I agree that you do have a problem now that your star witness is dead."

"If we can't get any positive evidence, we might be able to bluff him into admitting something, or trying to run," O'Grady said. "Either one would be the kind of evidence I can use."

Tabitha wrote a note to Loughran and went outside and found a young boy who promised to deliver the note for the nickel she gave him. She watched him walk down the block to the courthouse, where he turned into the entrance.

O'Grady sat in a chair behind the open door into the darkness of the back room. From there he could watch the counter yet not be seen, and he could hear the conversation.

Less than an hour after Tabitha wrote the note, she saw the sheriff himself walk into the store. She finished weighing out a five-pound sack of rolled oats for Mrs. Wilson and then turned to the tall man waiting to see her.

O'Grady had forgotten how thin the man was, and the close-cut beard gave his lean face a sinister look. But it was the cold green eyes that held a person's attention.

"Miss Rothmore, you mentioned in your note that Torris Canatale had been to see you recently. I'm sorry to say he no longer works with the security services company. I'm not sure if he was killed in the attack on the town or not, but I suspect that is what happened. He was found dead in the prairie a short time ago.

"Anyway, I'll be more than happy to tell you what he must have told you. This is a legitimate firm that offers special protection to merchants, a kind of civilian guard force that keeps tabs on its members. Entirely legitimate and legal. Now, if you're interested, we can set you up on a year's contract for two dollars a day. That includes Sundays and holidays, of course."

"That's what Mr. Canatale told me. But I did have some questions. Did he own the company, or is it a separate operation or is it partly owned by you? I just don't understand your connection."

"Oh, no, no. I'm just stepping in to help out a friend who was killed. A tragedy. He and his partner, another merchant here in town who is listed as a silent partner, own the business."

"Sheriff, that's interesting, because I was talking to some of the other merchants who belong, and they tell me that you were the one who contacted them, six or eight months ago. You told them it was a little sideline you had started."

The sheriff frowned. "Are you cross-examining me here, Miss Rothmore?'

"Land sakes, of course not! Just curious. I want to be sure that reliable people are handling the security of my store. I insist on knowing who owns the company and who works for it. As simple as that."

"Well, this is unusual. I'll talk to the remaining partner and see if he'll consent to those terms."

"Another thing bothers me. I have an uncle in Chicago, and he tells me that his store there has the same kind of protection. But he said the men were criminals, and if the merchants didn't pay the money, a bunch of thugs came in and broke up the store. He said they were paying the protection money to the criminals so they wouldn't damage their stores."

"I know little about Chicago. I can assure you that nothing like that has ever happened here."

"Well, there I'll have to differ with you. One man said he refused the protection and that night his front window was smashed in and half his store destroyed. Yesterday I refused Mr. Canatale's offer of protection, and last night three men broke into my store through the front window. One of them died in the window and the other was shot full of double-ought buck. Sheriff, how can there be any difference between this and Chicago?"

Sheriff Loughran snorted. "Miss, I resent the implication."

"Then you deny that you sent those men here last night with Torris Canatale to smash up my store?"

"I most certainly do deny it."

"But you can't, because Torris told me that you instructed him to do just that."

"Convenient of you to say, now that the man is dead. You plan on sitting guard inside your store every night from now on? That's what it will take. Those same men might be back. I won't put up with this kind of talk. If you want the protection, you'll pay for it. Otherwise, you take your chances."

'The same way my father did? Is that why you hung him from the front of the store, because he was trying to get the other merchants to quit paying you money each month, Sheriff? This is your protection racket, and you're a murderer. You also had Torris and his three friends kill the U.S. marshal who came here to look into my father's killing.''

"Shut up! I don't have to listen to this.''

"But you haven't denied it.''

"I don't need to.''

O'Grady stepped out from the back room, the double-barreled shotgun in his hands, the hammers back.

"I think you do need to listen, Sheriff. Because I'm arresting you for the murder of Stanley Rothmore, and for the murder and complicity in murder of U.S. Marshall J. B. Tippit.''

The sheriff snorted. "Who the hell are you to be arresting me?''

"I'm a United States justice agent, and you're under arrest.''

The sheriff moved faster than O'Grady figured he would. He leapt to Tabitha, grabbed her before she could move, and pulled her in front of him.

"Go ahead, Justice Agent. Use the scatter-gun. All you'll do is kill this little lady. I'm going out the back door. If I see it open a crack in the next five minutes, Miss Rothmore here gets her head blown off with the derringer in my pocket. Come out here and put down that weapon.''

"So you admit you killed the lady's father.''

"Hell, no, and you can't prove it.'' He dragged Tabitha as he shuffled toward the door to the rear of the store, through it, and out to the back door.

"Remember, Agent, don't even try to follow us or this small one is dead meat for the undertaker. Understand?''

"Yeah, I hear you,'' O'Grady said, lowering the shotgun. When Sheriff Loughran went out the back door, Canyon put the bar across, locking it, then he grabbed the rifle he had picked up that morning and the shells and rushed to the front door. He snapped a night lock, turned the closed sign around, and ran out. He picked the short end of the street to the cross street where he could see into the alley and ran as fast as he could.

By the time he got to the alley, he saw the sheriff riding down the street half a block away, with Tabitha in her light-blue dress clutched in front of him.

O'Grady looked at the hoofprints the horse had made. Evidently the sheriff had stolen it from the alley. There wasn't another horse in sight.

Canyon ran the block to the livery stable and yelled for the stable boy to help him saddle Cormac. They saddled the mount in record time and O'Grady was in the leather and riding a few moments later. He charged back to the alley and leaned out of the saddle, looking at the hoofprints. It was an easy trail to follow here. The sheriff would keep to the back less-traveled streets to avoid a public display. Where was he going? What could he do? He had as much as admitted the charges by running.

Now all O'Grady had to do was track him down, rescue Tabitha, and take his ex-gunman and outlaw and now sheriff into custody. That was all.

Canyon bent lower, followed the tracks across the next street, and saw that the trail was leading out of town, angling for the small stream that ran to the east, toward Missouri. At least they were working upstream.

O'Grady didn't think what might happen to Tabitha. He stepped down from Cormac and made sure he was on the right trail, then he rode harder. I'm coming Tabitha, I'm coming!

17

The trail that Canyon O'Grady followed riding Cormac changed directions twice, and seemed to make no sense. Sheriff Loughran was at least a mile, perhaps two ahead of O'Grady now and he had only the hoof prints in the Kansas prairie to guide him.

Once the trail turned back toward town; then, after a hundred yards, it went east again. Ahead two miles, he could see some buildings of a farm or a small ranch. The prints turned again and angled toward the buildings.

Loughran didn't have a rifle, but they probably had one that the sheriff could buy or steal at the farm ahead. He could see it was a farm now, with a big patch of rows of corn and what looked like a field of wheat.

He rode to the left, put the big barn between himself and the house, and charged forward quickly. Cormac responded to his knee pressure and jolted into a gallop, covering the ground to the barn quickly.

O'Grady tied Cormac behind the barn and went through a small rear door. He saw that the dun horse the sheriff rode was not there. Neither was it tied out front when O'Grady stared at the small farmhouse.

He came out of the barn and ran for the well house halfway to the clapboard residence. No shots tailed him.

"You looking for somebody, mister?" a youth asked from behind him. O'Grady whirled, saw the kid, and straightened.

"Did a man ride in here recently holding a woman on the horse with him?"

"Yes, sir. Got a drink, paid me fifteen dollars for that old rifle we had, and lit out like a scared rabbit to the east. Been gone, oh, about an hour by now, I'd say."

"The woman try to get away?"

"Sure as hell did. Said he was kidnapping her. He joshed her out of that, said she was always pulling jokes on him that way. Looks of things, though, I couldn't tell. My folks are in town buying some seed and some parts for the plow."

"You sure he went east?"

"Yes, sir. Dead east with the woman." The youth paused, doubt now tingeing his face. "Was she kidnapped?"

"Indeed she was, and now the bastard has a rifle. Going to make my job harder."

"Look, I didn't know, I—"

O'Grady waved him off. "You have a canteen I could carry some water in?"

"Yes, sir."

"You get it while I get my horse."

Five minutes later, O'Grady had found the prints heading east. They had the same wide shoes, same depth of a two-rider load. They cut across the corner of a wheat field, then into virgin prairie again going east.

Ahead about two miles he saw a creek. Loughran must know O'Grady was tracking him by this time. The man would set up an ambush. He'd kill off his tracker, rape Tabitha and then kill her, and he could ride back into town free and still be sheriff and take his time getting his assets turned into cash so he could move before another U.S. agent showed up.

The tracks angled dead-center on a heavy growth of trees and brush around a creek a half-mile ahead. Ideal spot for an ambush. When O'Grady knew for sure that the trail would hit the brush, he turned off and galloped Cormac a quarter of a mile toward the brush line, then he cantered into the cover and concealment of the woods along the creek.

The brush barely masked him here, but now he worked forward, quickly aiming for the heaviest section of the brush. What would Loughran do now? He would know his ambush was discovered. Would he hold his hidden position and wait for O'Grady to work up toward him, hoping for a killing first shot?

That's what O'Grady would do in the same spot. Loughran was no tenderfoot. He'd been Texas-trained and a fast gun in the big state.

When O'Grady figured he and Cormac were three hundred yards from the spot where the trail crossed into the heavy brush, he stopped and stepped out of the saddle. He took the rifle, made sure it had a round in chamber and that he had another twenty rounds in his pockets. Then he worked forward through the brush.

He wasn't an Indian, but he had trained with one, and he slipped from one cover to another so quietly it would take an expert to pick up any noise.

After two hundred yards he rested and listened. He could see nothing through the heavy brush of willow and wild roses and chokecherry and a few tall cottonwoods. Where was Loughran? What had he done with Tabitha?

O'Grady stepped forward again, making sure that each made no noise, broke no branch, that he let no branch snap back.

"No! Stop it!"

The voice came through plainly but distant. It had to be Tabitha. What was he doing to her?

O'Grady moved out faster, rushed twenty yards in one surge to a large cottonwood ahead. He looked up the trunk. The tree would be easy to climb. He decided against it. It would limit his mobility. He could be a chicken in the tree ready for shooting.

Ten minutes later he had crept another fifty yards

forward. He could see the dun horse now in the edge of some heavy brush. Where was Sheriff Loughran?

Brush moved to his left. He watched the spot until he saw it tremble as if someone crept through below the tops. He saw a flash of color as the sheriff's shirt showed through, then was gone.

Canyon couldn't just start shooting. He had to know where Tabitha was, first. Damn.

He moved forward again. The brush he had seen moving now was motionless. Then a spike-tailed grouse lifted off from the brush to the right of the clothes flash. The bird's fast wingbeat sounded like a train going past, then the bird cleared the growth and sailed off silently.

O'Grady concentrated on the spot where the bird had been flushed. It wouldn't move unless someone came within two or three feet of where it hid crouched under some growth.

Movement!

A soft cry that came muffled. He'd gagged her. Surprise was still O'Grady's best weapon. He angled toward the new direction. His knee hit a hand-size rock and he lifted it, grinned, and stood up behind a cottonwood and lofted the rock over the brush and ahead to the left. He crouched and watched for movement when the rock smashed through the drying-out brush.

He was still this side of the dun horse.

The rock crashed into the brush and he heard a grunt of surprise ahead to the left. Then a rifle shot exploded in the prairie silence and wisps of blue powder smoke drifted up into the brush.

Yeah! Not more than twenty feet ahead, slightly to the left, beside that big cottonwood.

Canyon edged forward slowly, without a sound. Every nerve ending in his body was primed and ready, on alert for any sound or movement from the suspect's position.

The noise was almost nonexistent; a whisper of a sound that caught his attention and he stared at a spot slightly to the left of the base of the big tree. Slowly a shoe edged into view, then a calf and at least a knee. A man's leg!

Without waiting to consider it, O'Grady lifted the rifle and sighted in on the knee. The sound of his rifle round exploding hit the brushy area like a cannon shot.

O'Grady saw the round slam into the sheriff's knee. At the same time he heard a billowing scream of pain and hatred. The leg vanished.

"Now, Tabitha! Run if you can. He's hurt. Run away!" Canyon pulled back behind a thin row of inch-thick saplings and prayed that Loughran hadn't taken a shotgun from the farm as well. Two revolver shots barked into the morning quiet. Both rounds went well over O'Grady's head and to the left.

He started to aim at the smoke pall in front of him but stopped. He didn't know where Tabitha was.

"Back off, O'Grady. I've got the girl. I'll kill her if you make another move."

"Go ahead, Loughran, then you won't have a hostage and I'll blow the whole damn area apart with lead. I'll find you easily and watch you die slowly as I chop your body up with a thousand slashes. You know about that, Loughran? It's when the Indians cut a victim often and long, slicing every part of his body, inflicting more pain than any white man ever thought possible. You won't die from the cuts, eventually you'll die from loss of blood. You want that?"

Canyon heard movement again.

"O'Grady! He's gone! Running, limping."

It was Tabitha. He believed her. She wouldn't say that to get him into danger. He charged through the brush, the weapon up and ready to fire. He broke through and saw the man at the far edge of a light stretch of brush twenty yards away reaching for the horse.

"Stop or you're dead," O'Grady yelled.

Sheriff Loughran looked up, lifted his rifle, and the big Irishman fired. The round jolted into Loughran's upper left shoulder, smashed the joint, and dumped him to the ground near the pawing, wild-eyed horse.

The animal was still tied to the tree. Its eyes went all white, then the mare reared up on its hind quarters to fight off any real or imagined threat. It screamed out a warning, then came down, tried to avoid the creature below it, but couldn't. Its shod hooves came down sharply with the fifteen hundred pounds of her body weight behind them.

One struck Loughran's chest before he could roll away. The last hoof coming down hit the sheriff's forehead, smashing downward, slicing his skull into two parts.

Tabitha turned away and screamed in terror, then she threw up where she was tied on the ground.

Canyon stared at the corpse of the dead lawman a moment, then walked forward, talking to the horse, calming it, patting its neck, untying it and leading it away from the stink of death that assaulted its nostrils. He tied the mount to some brush and ran to Tabitha.

"Oh, God, I'm going to be sick again." She turned away from him and retched as he held her forehead.

Canyon untied her and helped her stand. Then her arms went around him and she cried. Huge tears worked down her cheeks, and her chest heaved with the sobs that ground through her to try to cleanse some of the terror from her mind.

"Terrible! It was so terrible. He was alive one minute, then the hooves came down and he . . ."

O'Grady lifted her chin and wiped the tears from her eyes. He kissed her forehead and held her tightly again.

Three hours later, Tabitha had taken a bath, dressed, and insisted on opening the store. "I've got to be there for people who need things," she said, her chin thrust out in that stubborn attitude O'Grady had seen before.

He hugged her gently, then went out the front door to the sheriff's office. He found Deputy Pendleton and had a long talk with him. At last the deputy took a deep breath.

"Sure, I guess I can take over until a sheriff is elected. Not a lot to do. Our courts aren't working, as you probably know."

"I'll talk to the county officials and get you named interim sheriff. Nothing says you can't run for election when the election is called. You know now about the sheriff's sideline. I just hope you don't try anything like that."

"No, sir! I want nothing to do with any protection racket. I'd heard rumors, but nobody would talk freely. Not after Mr. Rothmore was found hung."

"So, you can clear off your books the unsolved murder of Rothmore and U.S. Marshal J. B. Tippit. The killers were Harry Loughran and Torris Canatale. I'll be in town for a day or two in case you want to ask any questions."

"Yes, sir," the deputy said. "A pleasure to meet you. Never known a lawman from the federal government before."

They shook hands and O'Grady walked out to Main Street.

It wasn't four o'clock yet. Nothing like being early for a date. He went to the hotel to Meg Ryson's room and knocked. There was a wait, then her voice came.

"Yes, who is it?"

When she heard his voice, she opened the door at once. She was nearly dressed. "You're a little early," she said. She stood there in her chemise and petticoat.

"You've never looked better." He bent and kissed her cheek.

"You better do more than that," she said.

"First, business. My work is done here."

She smiled "Actually I'm doing some work for the government, too. Some people in the Justice Department don't want Kansas to go slave. It's all unofficial of course. They're calling it a covert operation. Doesn't that sound good?"

"I work through the Justice Department also, but I get my assignments directly from President Buchanan."

Meg lifted her brows. "I am impressed. That's about a hundred miles above my authorization. I brought fifty thousand dollars with me to raise a fighting company and do battle with the armed bands of the pro-slavery groups. So far so good."

"You're convinced that Buckeye Springs is safe now for the North?"

"More than safe. We won't have any more trouble with the southern sympathizers now in this area. Smithson was the leader of the southern night riders. He was one of the casualties and we burned his ranch to the ground. It had been set up by the pro-slavers three years ago."

"Did the North have a night-rider captain in town?"

"Of course! The barber, of all men. He did a good job, if a little on the wild side. I've ordered him to stop all violent activity. Now he becomes a talker, a diplomat. We don't need the burning and bleeding now. We need to get the rest of the solid citizens on our side."

O'Grady watched her. "So you'll be moving on?"

"Back to Lawrence. I've got a house there, a kind of office."

"You going to get dressed or keep teasing me with your sexy, half-draped body?"

"I had my bath and my nap." She lifted the chemise until it showed both of her jiggling breasts. "We could just stay here for a while."

O'Grady bent and kissed her breasts. Her hands played with his flame-red hair and she sighed.

He stood, his hands holding her breasts. "Or you could cover up your marvelous parts and we could go get the best meal in town. A kind of celebration."

She reached in and kissed him. "Then we could come back here and continue the celebration? Here or in your room."

"I like that. I'm getting hungry."

Two hours later they came back to his room from a leisurely supper at Delmonico's Restaurant, which had the best steak in town.

"Oh, I've got some good eating and drinking things in my room. I'll be right back."

He went with her to carry them.

"Where's the nearest telegraph?" he asked her.

She frowned. "Probably up near Lawrence. Kansas City, for sure. They're stringing the wires westward. I'm not sure how far they are. The company says they'll have the wires all the way to San Francisco by 1862."

"Four more years?"

In his room they sat on the bed and began undressing each other. They had locked the door but didn't put a chair under the doorknob. No one was after them now.

Meg took off his shirt and cried out in surprise. "You're wounded!"

A blood line from Torris' knife showed across his upper chest.

"It's only a scratch."

"But your arm!"

"More than a scratch. I bound it up. It will heal. Forget it."

She kissed his sliced chest, then the bandage over his arm cut.

Canyon bent and kissed her bare breasts, then he heard something at the door. A key turned in the lock and the door swung open. Tabitha backed in carrying a large paper sack. She closed the door and then turned around, holding a room key.

"Surprise," she said. The word died in her throat as she saw the two nearly naked people sitting on the bed.

"Oh, damn," she said softly. "Looks like I've done it again. I figured you'd be here. I also figured Meg might be here." She grinned. "Come on, O'Grady, this is a small town and I'm not exactly blind, you know."

She set the sack on the dresser and took off her jacket and then unbuttoned her blouse.

"I'm not only sighted; I'm broad-minded and don't mind sharing," Tabitha said.

Neither O'Grady nor Meg had been able to say a word yet. They sat there staring at her.

Tabitha pulled off her blouse and there was nothing under it. "Sharing, a good old-fashioned trait. I like it. I'm willing to share if you are, Meg. We can even compare notes on his performance. Hey, have both of you gone dumb on me here?"

O'Grady chuckled.

Meg looked at him. "You've been with her before, I'd guess." Meg shrugged. "What the hell, I think it might be fun." She looked at Tabitha. "Do we give him a vote?"

"Not in this room! It's strictly up to us. He doesn't have a vote here, we do. And I think we both voted with a yes." Tabitha turned and pushed the chair under the doorknob and moved over to the bed. She bent and kissed Canyon hard on the mouth and sat down on his free side.

Meg looked at Tabitha. "We're going to spoil this one rotten, you know that. First thing you know he'll want two girls every time he feels sexy."

"Maybe not," Tabitha said, grinning. She slipped out of her skirt and kicked off her shoes so she was totally naked. "Maybe if we tire him out so bad he can't even crawl out of bed in the morning, he'll learn his lesson not to play one beautiful, sexy woman off against another beautiful, sexy woman."

Meg frowned. "Might work. Let's try!"

They both pounced on Canyon and pushed him backward on the bed.

Telegram? Was he thinking about a telegram? It could wait a few days. He was eager to see if the two beautiful females could get him that exhausted. At least it would be an interesting experiment!

KEEP A LOOKOUT!

**The following is the opening section from the
next novel in the action-packed new
Signet Western series
CANYON O'GRADY**

CANYON O'GRADY #9

COUNTERFEIT MADAM

August 4, 1860, Minneapolis, Minnesota

Canyon O'Grady stared at the man on the floor with
two bullet holes in his chest. He fit the description:
small man with handlebar mustache, bald, and wearing spectacles. O'Grady's only lead to the ring coun-
terfeiting U.S. Treasury Bonds, Rufus J. Thorndike,
lay on the floor cold, stiff, and terribly dead.

O'Grady had seen enough bodies to know that
Thorndike had been dead at least six hours. He decided he'd better do some quick looking now before
the sheriff came.

Rufus Thorndike had been shot twice in the chest,
so close the powder burns showed. He'd probably died
instantly from the one round through his heart. A small
desk to one side had been thoroughly searched. The
hunt must have been quick, messy, and unsuccessful.
Papers had been scattered; pigeon holes in the front
of the rolltop had been emptied and their contents
dumped on the desk.

Several certificates lay on the floor. They were
stocks good for one hundred shares each. Robbery

hadn't been the motive. What had the killer been looking for? Perhaps the same thing O'Grady was searching for: the name of the man printing the counterfeit U.S. Treasury Bonds.

A pad of paper half covered by the mess on the desk showed a string of small pictures, basic sketches anyone might make. He looked at them again. They formed a pictograph. The first showed a fish, then a falls. Next came a half moon with stars around it and a small boat and two stick figures.

O'Grady looked at it and nodded. Rufus must have hoped that he and another man could go fishing one night at the falls in a two-man boat. The pictograph was easy to decipher.

But that wasn't much help in his search. He found three more of the picture messages, one describing a night of love and passion with a woman with long, dark hair. He skipped the others and kept looking for a clue. Rufus had discovered the fake bonds and had sent one to Washington, and O'Grady had hoped that Rufus would have some idea as to which printer had done them and who the culprit might be.

If Rufus knew he wasn't going to tell, unless he'd left a note, a message on his desk in writing. A file, perhaps. A small file drawer in the desk produced nothing helpful.

O'Grady sat in the dead man's desk chair and rocked back. Where would I hide information like that if I was scared? Sure, I'd hide it in my brain, but where else? O'Grady powered his imagination into high gear for a pretending game.

Where? How? The two questions. In the office, at the desk probably, but how? He looked back at the two pictographs he had skipped. No luck.

Squares of paper had been tacked to a six-foot-long bulletin board on the wall beside the desk. A handwritten message on one reminded Rufus that he needed to go to the dentist on Tuesday. He wouldn't make it.

Another note had a date and a time, three days hence at seven-thirty. A third square of paper displayed a rough sketch of the head and shoulders of the dark-haired woman. A date, perhaps?

O'Grady stood up and paced the room. He was looking at things the wrong way. He went as far from the desk and note wall as he could get and stared at them. Small notes were everywhere. Rufus had been a visually activated man. If he could see a note he wouldn't forget the event.

O'Grady looked back at the note wall. The squares of paper were of various colors. He hadn't picked up on that before. The man had written everything important on paper. So where was the name and address of the counterfeiter?

Now he looked more closely at the colors of the papers. There was a rough line of light blue paper, with a half-dozen five-by-seven-inch sheets tacked to the board. But there were other notes and colors interspersed. He studied only the blue pages.

Taking them in order meant nothing: a lodge meeting time, the date of an appointment with his banker, a note to call the pastor before church Sunday, a figure of $20, a list of food to buy. The last one was a fishing date for Saturday.

He tried switching the order. Still nothing had anything to do with money except the $20. Not good enough. He went back to the far wall and looked again. He found five notes on soft red paper on the wall, again with papers of other colors between the sheets.

The red papers made up a strange collection: One sketch showed a river falls, another a building with lumber around it. The third was ten lines drawn in two sets of five with the fifth and tenth lines crossing the other four. The next-to-last red sheet had a drawing of a kerosene lamp with red rays, done in crayon, coming from it. The last red sheet showed nothing but a sun peeking over the horizon and two arrows.

Excerpt from COUNTERFEIT MADAM

O'Grady felt a tingle. This was it, this was what Rufus would have told him if he had lived. Quickly now, O'Grady went to the note wall and took the thumbtacks from the five sheets of red paper, folded them, and put them securely into his inside jacket pocket. Then he walked out of the house and closed the door. He figured someone else would find Rufus before too long.

He walked two blocks to the Minnesota River. There was a falls here somewhere. Yes, on Minnehaha Creek, the famous Minnehaha Falls immortalized by Henry Wadsworth Longfellow in his epic poem *Song of Hiawatha,* published five years ago.

But there were other falls around as well. They provided power for the grain mills and the lumber mills. So he had the falls and the sawmills. What did the ten marks mean? Ten bonds? Had Rufus known of ten bogus bonds, or could it be ten outlets, ten salesmen in ten cities around the country?

The lamp with the red rays meant nothing to him at all. Was it a rising or setting sun? What did the arrows mean? One went up toward the top of the page, the other pointed to the right.

O'Grady walked along A Street and saw a large sawmill, a pond, and stacks of drying lumber to the north. He walked to the south, downstream on the river, and soon saw another mill. Both used the river falls for power. But they weren't ten miles from town or one another. He was stumped.

He wandered north to the business section and turned down Main Street. He went into a small café just this side of Minnesota Street and asked for a cup of coffee. Spreading out the sheets of paper on a table, he studied them again.

When the young waitress brought his coffee, she looked at the papers with surprise.

"Do you like picture puzzles, too? I just love them. Mr. Thorndike likes to play games that way. He used to come in once in a while and he'd give me a pictograph for his order. Once as a joke I brought him a whole uncooked chicken on a plate.''

She was maybe eighteen—open, friendly, not jaded yet.

''Did he come in here often?''

''He used to; then a couple of weeks ago he said he was going to stay indoors. He thought somebody was following him. Haven't seen him now in a while. You know what that picture puzzle says?''

''No, A friend gave it to me and I'm stumped. A water falls, a sawmill, ten of something, a lamp and a sunrise maybe, because one arrow points upward. I don't know about the other arrow.''

''Mmm. Let me see. Sometimes Mr. Thorndike would put them on different pieces of paper this way and mix up the order so it would be harder to figure. That might be the same here. Let's see. It's something about a sawmill at a river falls, that's for sure. 'Course we got falls and rivers and sawmills all over the place, even all the way to the St. Croix River over to the east edge of the state.''

The girl grinned. ''Well, that could be. You take the sunrise picture and put it first, then the river and the falls and the sawmill. Biggest sawmill operations to the east of us is all the way out to Stillwater on the St. Croix River. There's a falls there that powers lots of sawmills.''

''You think it might refer to Stillwater, rather than a Minneapolis sawmill?''

''Oh, yeah. Why else put in the sunrise and the arrows to the east? See, on a map the top is always north and the bottom south, so when you face north, east is on your right. And the sun rises in the east. Yep, I definitely think that's the first part of the picture puzzle. The other two don't give me any ideas at all.''

The waitress grinned again. ''You want anything else, a doughnut maybe, or a piece of home-baked cherry pie?''

''I'll try the pie.''

Her smile brightened the café. "Good! You'll like it. Made it myself." She leaned closer to look at the sketches again. "Lordy, I just can't figure out that ten or the lamp. Stillwater is maybe twenty miles over east."

She straightened up. "I'll fetch that pie."

When she brought back the pie she propped her chin in her hands and studied the five pictures again. She shook her head.

"Glory, I just can't figure. They don't go together easy like most of those I see. Is it important?"

"Friendly little bet. I could lose five dollars."

"In that case, I'll think on it. The lamp with the red beams tickles my fancy somewhere, but I can't quite remember what it means or where it is. I might. You stop by for supper."

O'Grady finished the pie and coffee, waved at the young girl, and ambled down the street. He walked into the county sheriff's office in the rough-hewn wood-frame courthouse and found the man in. Two assistants and three deputies were in the office. O'Grady persuaded one of the deputies that he needed to see the boss.

His name was Sheriff Longtree, and he wasn't smiling.

"I'm busy today, just found a man shot in his own office. Terrible. No clues but some powder burns. What's your complaint?"

"No complaint, Sheriff. More like a puzzle. Trying to find a friend of mine and all he left me were these five drawings." O'Grady spread them out on the lawman's desk.

"Hell, I don't have time to play games. You might talk to Melvin out front. He plays with pictographs sometimes. Used to drive me crazy with them."

O'Grady found Melvin, and the man's eyes sparkled.

"Love these things. Any order?"

O'Grady shook his head.

Melvin studied them. "The obvious are easy, but what is the ten for, and the sunrise?" He looked at the lamp and the red rays. "I've never seen one in color before, those red rays. Yeah, there is one place nearby that the sheriff tells me the whores are hanging red lamps in their windows when they're looking for customers. A kind of "ready for you" sign. Sheriff says he's calling it a red-light house. Think that's important?"

"Could be," O'Grady said. "Just where is this place with the red lights?"

"Oh, not in Minneapolis. It's in Stillwater, eighteen, twenty miles to the east."

O'Grady nodded. A sudden shiver hit him and he tried not to let it show. That pretty much tied it down to Stillwater, which had to be his next stop. He let the deputy play with the pictures for a while, then shuffled them together.

"Thanks a lot. Maybe I'll get a sudden inspiration over a tall glass of whiskey."

Outside, O'Grady walked down the street looking for a stage. He found the stage office, but no trips to Stillwater were scheduled until the next noon. O'Grady didn't want to wait that long. He wished he had Cormac there, but the big palomino stallion with the pale bronze coat and white tail and mane was resting somewhere outside of Denver. There had been no time to get him to Minnesota.

At the hotel, O'Grady packed what little he had taken out of his carpet bag and walked to the livery, where he hired a horse and saddle. A half hour later he was on his way to Stillwater. He wasn't sure what he would find when he got there, but at least he had some clues.

It was three in the afternoon when he headed out. If he didn't get lost he should get to the town on the St. Croix River sometime around eight that evening.

The blood bay he had chosen from the livery was lively enough and deep-chested, so O'Grady let her out a little now and then to see what she could do. He hadn't brought anything to eat, so the cherry pie had to last him until he got into the sawmill hamlet. The livery man had said that Stillwater's residents numbered no more than a thousand souls if you counted all the baby goats.

It was eight-thirty and dark when he rode down the muddy street and checked out the buildings of Stillwater. They were all structured of rough-sawn lumber from the resident lumber mills. Made you feel as if the whole town could burn down in about thirty seconds.

There were the usual general stores and saloons, a hardware store and a tinsmith. Nowhere did he see a sign for a lawyer, or a stock-and-bond salesman, or an investment broker.

He passed one hotel that had been built just slightly off square, then chose another frame-building hotel four doors down—The Lumberman's Hotel, which had only two stories and a small restaurant he spotted past the lobby. O'Grady registered and learned that the dining room would be closing in a half hour, so he went in and had a meal before they threw the leftover food away. He ate and then stashed his gear in Room 24, second floor front.

O'Grady had passed one sawmill on his way into town. It was on a crook in the river and smoke billowed and engines barked and they were just about through for the day.

The smell of wood smoke was everywhere. He guessed not a shovelful of coal was ever burned in this town. They had plenty of bark and edges and slab wood as well as the ends off the trim saw to fire five hundred wood stoves and fireplaces.

It was nine-thirty, and this might be a good time to check in at the local gossip mill, if the barbershop was still open. It wasn't. He'd try it tomorrow. He headed for the biggest saloon he could see. It was Aces High across the street and two doors down from his hotel. Inside he saw what he expected.

Aces High was a gambling-drinking-whoring saloon, with a fancy staircase that led along one wall to the second floor, where he guessed there were a dozen cribs for handy use. The girls didn't pose prettily in some salon upstairs. Instead they worked the tables, served drinks, and had their bottoms pinched.

It was a rugged kind of saloon, not given to fancy mirrors or expensive furniture. The plank floor was chewed up with the tracks of hobnail boots used by loggers and pond men. Sturdy wooden chairs bellied up to square solid tables. Drunks didn't smash through tables here; instead they bounced off and hit the floor.

O'Grady went to the bar, bought a beer for a dime, and sat at the side of the saloon with his back to the wall. No sense in taking any silly chances. As he sipped the beer, O'Grady watched and listened.

The talk was all logging and lumbering, chopping down trees and sawing them into boards.

A slender dance-hall girl leaned over his table and stared.

"Hey, you're new in town. I'd never miss that red hair. It's hot enough to start a fire. See anything you like?"

As she leaned over, the bodice of her low-cut dance-hall dress billowed out and allowed a clear view down to her navel. Her breasts were bare and one-hand size.

She let him have a good look, then sat down across from him.

"Make you happy for just a lousy two dollars," she said. "Oh, I'm Patsy."

"Patsy, I'm not buying, but I'll set you up to a watered whiskey and we can talk."

"Beer, I'm a beer drinker." She went to the bar and came back with one for herself and a fresh one for him. She pocketed the quarter he gave her and sipped the beer.

"So what do we talk about?"

"Ten," he said.

"Pardon me?"

"Ten, does that number mean anything special here in town?"

"Ten what?"

"That's what I don't know. An old friend gave me a puzzle to figure out. I can't figure what the ten stands for."

"Hey, you're supposed to have a brain, lumberjack. Me, I just got a body. You want to buy it tonight or not?"

"Broke, sweetheart. If you don't need the two bucks, I'll be glad to run upstairs switching your cute little ass all the way."

Patsy snorted, then grinned. "Hell, I'm half tempted to do it." She traced a finger around his jawline. "I ain't seen a handsome bunch of man like you in this dump in a damn long time." She stood, pulled in a deep breath, and slowly shook her head.

"Truth is, I can't afford it, and I'd get my ass whacked good and proper for wasting my time and not making any cash money for the bastard who pushes us. Try me again when I'm a little bit drunk." She took the beer and hurried toward a table where two young men had just sat down.

"Young feller, could I bother you for the use of a chair?"

O'Grady looked up at the older man who stood beside the table. He was well into his sixties and held two mugs of beer, one in each hand. He winked one greenish eye.

"Hell, what I really want is to sit down and talk. 'Bout what I do best anymore is talk. You busy, stranger? I sure ain't seen you around town before."

O'Grady motioned to the chair. "Sit, rest yourself.

I'd be glad to talk. What I don't get enough of. You're right, I just hit town. You can fill me in on the local politics, how the wind is blowing, and where the bodies are buried. You up to all that?''

"On only two beers?" the old timer asked with a laugh that sailed high into the loftier ranges.

"That won't be a problem," O'Grady said. "This here looks like a sawmill town, pure and simple."

"Hell if it ain't. Oh, my manners. Name's Ira, I been here since Hector was a weanling. Yep, we chop and drag and saw. Do a lot of floating, too. 'Course, now that gets more expensive."

"How many mills here?"

"Two that 'mount to anything. Biggest is the Rombold Lumber Company. Three brothers in their thirties run the place. They ain't the woodsmen their father was. He started the outfit. Rombold drags a lot of weight hereabouts. Employs more than half the timber workers in town."

"The other one is smaller?"

"By about four times. It's the Norgard Sawmilling and Lumber Company. I've worked for both of them. Still on the Norgard payroll. It's the class of the pair."

Ira tipped the beer he'd been working on. His brown eyes looked up and locked on O'Grady. "So, you're out of questions already?"

"How is the law here?"

"Sheriff Rex Spurlock . . . elected sheriff of Washington County. Good man. I'd trust him at my back in a shootout."

"Does the number ten have any special meaning in Stillwater?" O'Grady asked.

"Ten? Hell's bells! Ten what? Ten pennies in a dime? Ten dimes in a dollar? What the hell you mean, ten?"

"I don't know. Friend of mine gave me a puzzle to figure out and ten is part of it."

Ira shook his head. His white hair sailed from side to side and came to a rest only when he stopped.

"Nope, no such thing as an important 'ten' in Stillwater. I been here for thirty years, I should know."

"Then you must know all the best whores in town."

"Darn tootin'! We used to have one we called Fat Maud."

"What's the biggest whorehouse in town now?" O'Grady asked.

"Be the Charity House. Charity is the madam. Runs a nice clean place. Now Charity is a little chunky, but not really *fat*."

They talked for a half hour more. O'Grady bought the old man another beer and then headed outside. A piano recital had just finished on the other side of the street as O'Grady came out of the saloon.

A man and a woman stepped gingerly off the boardwalk into the muddy street. A buggy rolled toward them at a leisurely pace.

Without warning the horse neighed and darted forward, jerking the reins out of the startled driver's hands. The horse bolted ahead in panic, a runaway.

The rig headed directly at the man and woman in mid-street. The man lunged forward to save his companion, but he slipped and fell into the street on his stomach. The woman rushed ahead six steps, looked at the rampaging horse, and froze.

O'Grady had stopped at the edge of the boardwalk in front of the saloon. Now he darted into the muddy street, charging toward the woman, who didn't seem able to move. Her companion got to his feet, then slipped and fell again, sitting down in more mud.

O'Grady raced forward, hoping he could get to the woman before the horse ran her down. He had another ten feet to go. It would be close.

"Run, lady, run! Get out of there!" O'Grady bellowed.

But his words had no effect on the woman. She screamed as she watched the charging horse, but she couldn't move.